"I see you're making yourself at home."

Travis walked over to the sink, peeling off his T-shirt. "I don't want you and the boy here. I thought I made that clear."

Presented with his naked muscular torso, Paige stood her ground, raised her chin and said, "Can't we talk this whole thing over in a civilized manner?"

"I don't feel civilized around you," he said, taking her chin in his hand.

"And kindly let go of my chin," she seethed. "Physical intimidation is the cheapest of tricks."

Immediately he did as she asked, but he let his hand draw lingeringly across her jawline and down her slender neck. Something must have flared in her eyes. He said silkily, "Another cheap trick, I admit, but it proves you don't feel any more civilized than I do."

SANDRA FIELD, once a biology technician, now writes full-time under the pen names of Jocelyn Haley and Jan MacLean. She lives with her son in Canada's Maritimes, which she often uses as a setting for her books. She loves the independent life-style she has as a writer. She's her own boss, sets her own hours, and increasingly there are travel opportunities.

Books by Sandra Field

Don't miss any of our special offers. Write to us at the following address for information on our newest releases.

Harlequin Reader Service
901 Fuhrmann Blvd., P.O. Box 1397, Buffalo, NY 14240
Canadian address: P.O. Box 603,
Fort Erie, Ont. L2A 5X3

SANDRA FIELD

ring of gold

Harlequin Books

TORONTO • NEW YORK • LONDON
AMSTERDAM • PARIS • SYDNEY • HAMBURG
STOCKHOLM • ATHENS • TOKYO • MILAN

Harlequin Presents first edition February 1990
ISBN 0-373-11242-4

Original hardcover edition published in 1989
by Mills & Boon Limited

PROLOGUE

'WOULD you mind repeating what you just said?' Paige asked with a careful lack of expression in her voice.

'Not at all.' Paige's friend Barbara took a leisurely sip of her Bloody Mary. 'I'd like you to take a five-year-old boy, who goes by the unlikely name of Eustace Percival Brent Renshaw, to a little place in northern British Columbia called Nelson's Landing, where you will deliver him to his father, Travis Brent Renshaw.'

'Not *the* Travis Renshaw?'

'If you mean the man who wrote that one marvellous book about five years ago, then wrote the scripts for two trashy movies before disappearing from sight, then yes, *the* Travis Renshaw.'

But the momentary interest had disappeared from Paige's face. 'The answer's no.'

Calmly Barbara signalled the waiter to take their orders. Paige requested a spinach salad, then remarked, 'It's nice to see you, Barb. How's the job?'

'Paige dear, I didn't invite you for lunch to talk about my job. I'm serious about this—er—proposition.'

'You can be as serious as you like. The answer's still no.'

'Why don't you at least let me fill in the details?'

'I have to be back at work in forty-five minutes.'

'That will be long enough. You see, the president of our company is the executor of the will of Travis Renshaw's late wife, Stephanie.' Barbara was a lawyer, who worked part-time for a prestigious firm of barristers

5

in the Nob Hill area of San Francisco, and part-time with legal aid in a very different area of the city; the contrast, she said, did her good. She and Paige had met in the legal aid office, a place Paige frequented fairly often because she was a social worker dealing with delinquent boys. 'Stephanie Renshaw has left her son of the triple-barrelled name in the guardianship of Travis Renshaw,' Barbara continued. 'A very straightforward request, although one gathers from the wording that there was no love lost between them. The catch is that Mr Renshaw lives in a village of less than two hundred people in the wilds of northern Canada.' Barbara took another swig of her drink. 'We had to get a special atlas from the library to even find the place.'

Paige grimaced at her friend. 'So what's the catch?' Write Mr Renshaw one of your very correct legal letters and tell him to come to San Francisco to get his son. It's not as if he couldn't afford to—they made a movie out of his book, he must be rolling in money.'

'Under the terms of the will we are required to deliver the boy to his father . . . You know Mr Deschamps, nothing else will do.' Mr Deschamps was the president of her firm, whose old-fashioned starched collars were symbolic of the rigidity of his principles. 'So he asked me to do it.'

'Do it, then,' said Paige as the waiter put their food in front of them with a discreet flourish.

'I can't. I'm in court every day for the next two weeks. So I suggested your name to Mr Deschamps and gave him a glowing description of your capabilities—in the end I had him wondering why he'd ever asked me when such a paragon as you was available.'

'You've got a nerve!'

Barbara leaned forward, her green eyes fastened on her

friend's face. 'I know I have. I acted on impulse, Paige. It seemed such a golden opportunity to get you away from your job, away from the city, and give you a bit of a holiday . . . they say that part of the north is exquisitely beautiful. Do say yes, Paige darling, it would do you the world of good.'

'Barbara, I have a job too, with commitments I can't get out of!'

'Yes, you can. You told me last week you had an extra person on staff all summer so the regulars could take holidays.'

'I can't leave my caseload in the hands of someone who doesn't even know the boys.'

'Try it for once.'

'No.'

Barbara leaned forward, her face very serious. 'We're getting to the heart of the matter now, aren't we? Do you know what your problem is, Paige? You're beginning to think you're God, that no one else can do the job as well as you can. That's a pretty dangerous point of view.'

'I don't think I'm God!' Paige's lustrous brown eyes reflected the hurt she was feeling. 'How can you say that, Barb? I love my job, I care about the boys, and I try to do the best I can. That's all.'

Barbara had given up any pretence of eating. 'It's not all, and you know it. Ever since Martie died——'

'Don't, Barb!'

'Your brother died two years ago, Paige, and you've been on the run ever since. You're trying to save the world and you're half killing yourself in the process. You used to be a beautiful woman—but look at you now. Your hair needs cutting, you have circles under your eyes, and I bet it's six months since you bought yourself as much as a new pair of tights.'

Paige poked at her salad. 'You're exaggerating,' she

retorted. 'I'm just trying to stop other boys from going along the route Martie went.'

'*You're* rationalising,' Barbara said relentlessly. 'The truth is that you're burnt out. Utterly exhausted. Not only are you no use to yourself, pretty soon you won't be any use to anyone else.'

Paige looked up, some of the old fire in her eyes. 'I don't understand this unwarranted attack! I thought you were my friend.'

'Darling, I am. That's why I'm saying this. You don't know how many times in the past few months I've bitten my tongue . . . I'm worried about you, Paige. Worried to death. You can't save the world! And no matter how many boys you keep off the streets, you can't bring Martie back.'

Sudden tears glistened on Paige's long brown lashes. Barbara covered her friend's hand with her own and urged, 'Please take this boy up to his father, Paige. Then rent a car and drive around the mountains up there—there's nothing like a few mountains to restore one's sense of proportion.'

Paige stared at her companion in frustration, seeing the spiky, very becoming hairdo, the flawless make-up, the tasteful expensive clothes. But she had also seen Barbara in jeans and an old sweatshirt in the shabby legal aid office downtown; and they had known each other for over three years. She said with complete honesty, 'I haven't got the energy for a holiday in an unfamiliar place, Barb. But do you know what kind of a holiday I'd like? Two weeks in my apartment with nothing to do but sleep.'

'You'd have to take the phone off the hook—you've got kids calling you at every hour of the day and night.'

'Two whole weeks to sleep,' Paige repeated dreamily. 'Sounds like heaven . . . I might even do a few things around the apartment. Paint the bookshelves. Wallpaper the bathroom. I've never really taken the time to make the place seem like home.'

'You'd have no trouble getting the time off; they must owe you months of overtime.'

'Not quite!' For the first time since they had sat down, Paige laughed, a laugh that made her eyes sparkle. 'Weeks, maybe—but not months. Barb, I'm going to do it—I'm going to take two weeks off.'

Barbara had not expected to win quite so easily. She raised her glass. 'To a well-earned holiday!'

Paige drank obediently, then tackled her salad with new appetite. 'I could go shopping, too. Because you're right, it's ages since I bought myself anything. I saw a gorgeous skirt the other day in a little boutique near Union Square, but I was on my way to see Pedro's teacher so I couldn't stop.'

Barbara did not want the conversation moving to Pedro, one of the more charming of Paige's misfits. 'And you will do that little favour for me, won't you?' she coaxed. 'You could fly up one day and come back the next, it wouldn't take long. I think it would be a good idea, get you out of the rut you're in and put you in the mood for a holiday.'

Paige frowned; to shepherd a small boy to the wilds of Canada was not her idea of the way to begin a vacation. 'Are you sure you can't get out of your court cases?'

'Positive.'

'Well, I guess I'll do it, then . . . I suppose if it weren't for you I wouldn't be taking a break at all.'

It was not an enthusiastic response, but Barbara knew Paige well enough to know it was a commitment, and that Eustace Percival Brent Renshaw would be delivered to his father as promptly as possible. 'Good,' she said. 'The firm will look after all your reservations. I'll let you know as soon as they're confirmed . . . and thanks, Paige.'

Now that the decision was made, Paige sounded much more gracious. 'You've done lots of favours for me over the years. Besides, it won't take long,' she said blithely.

'Promise me one thing? No, two.'

'Sure.'

'First, you won't even think about work for two weeks—and that includes Pedro.'

'Well, OK.'

'And secondly, you'll get your hair cut.'

Again Paige laughed, running her fingers through her russet hair. 'Promise,' she said.

Well satisfied, Barbara picked up the bill. 'You'll have to hurry, you've only got five minutes to get to work.'

Paige scrambled to her feet. 'And a million things to do when I get there.'

'Including a request for leave.'

'Yes, ma'am!' Impulsively Paige hugged her friend. 'You were absolutely right, I do need a vacation . . . I'm already looking forward to it. Thanks, Barb.'

'You're welcome. Although I wish you were taking it somewhere other than your apartment.'

Barbara's wish was to come true. But neither of them knew this, which for Paige's peace of mind, at least, was just as well.

CHAPTER ONE

EUSTACE PERCIVAL BRENT RENSHAW planted his leather-shod feet on the dirt road and announced, 'I don't like this place. I'm tired.'

Paige held tightly to her temper; she too was tired. They had flown from San Francisco to Vancouver early that morning, their flight to Whitehorse had been delayed, and a stopover in Fort St John had stretched into a two-hour wait in a hot and stuffy terminal. Consequently they had arrived in Whitehorse and picked up the rental car much later than Paige had planned. Then they had driven the eighty miles to Nelson's Landing.

She had stopped the car on the hill that overlooked the village and had climbed out. The streets were laid out in a grid, the old-fashioned wooden houses painted bright colours. But the settlement was dwarfed by the lake behind them, a huge, glacial lake encircled by mountains whose peaks stood out starkly against the evening sky. The lake was glazed with blue and gold, and the mountains seemed to glow with a light of their own. She had never seen anywhere more beautiful in her life.

Drive around the mountains, Barbara had said. They'll restore your sense of proportion.

Then her passenger clambered out of the car, patently unimpressed with the view, scrubbing at his eyes with sticky hands. He did look tired. Paige said quickly, 'We're in Nelson's Landing, Eustace. This is where your father lives.'

11

'I'm hungry.'

'You can have something to eat at your father's. But first I have to find out which house is his,' she replied with false cheer. 'I can see a petrol station and a couple of shops—we'll ask there. It's not a very big place, everyone must know everyone else. Let's go, Eustace.'

The boy kicked the nearest tyre. 'I hate that name!'

Inwardly Paige counted to ten; she had been calling him Eustace all day. Feeling her way, she asked, 'What did your mother call you?'

'She called me Eustace.'

Top of the class for tact, thought Paige. 'What would you like me to call you?'

'Eustace is a sissy name. I had a fight in playschool 'cause of my name.'

Paige gave him a considering look. He was a beautiful child, or would be if he ever smiled; with his overly long brown curls and huge violet eyes, she could see that he might have to fight to defend his masculinity. His clothing did not help his image. For a day in July he was outfitted in brown tweed shorts, jacket and cap, with brown knee socks that were sagging around his ankles and brown laced shoes. Although he looked like a child in a Victorian picture-book, his pugnacious little chin and wary expression defied either sympathy or amusement.

She said cheerfully, 'I'm not crazy about Percival, either.'

'Brent is OK.'

'Brent is a fine name. Let's make a deal. I'll call you Brent, if you'll call me Paige.' So far he had studiously avoided calling her anything at all.

'I gotta call you Miss Montgomery. The maid said so.'

The maid, a hatchet-faced woman, had delivered the boy into Paige's care what seemed like days ago. 'The maid's not here,' Paige said matter-of-factly, 'and I am. So it's Paige and Brent, all right? And now we'd better try and find your father's house.'

He glowered at her. 'I don't wanna go there!'

Torn between pity and exasperation, Paige said, 'Brent, you have to—he's your father.'

'I don't have a father. Only uncles.'

Pity won, for Paige knew enough about Stephanie Renshaw's life to imagine exactly who the uncles were. She knelt on the road, clasping the boy by the shoulders, and feeling them tense in rejection as she did so. 'This is your real father, Brent. You're going to live with him.'

'Don't want to.'

'He'll be good to you, I'm sure,' she said, hating herself for mouthing a platitude of whose truth she was quite unsure. 'And you'll like living up here—you'll see grizzly bears and caribou and all sorts of interesting things. It'll be more fun than the city.'

'I want my mother,' said Brent.

Wishing she could take him in her arms, Paige said gently, 'I'm sorry your mother is dead—it's hard, I know. But you do have a father, so that's something.' The violet eyes regarded her unwinkingly, refusing any consolation. Not envying Travis Renshaw the task of bringing up his son, she added, 'Let's go, chum.'

But as she herded him into the car she saw his lower lip stick out and his eyes dart this way and that with the air of a hunted animal. She closed his door and got in the car herself. 'Brent, it will be all right,' she said strongly. 'I've never met your father, but I read the book he wrote, and the person who wrote that book has to have a lot of good in him.' The same man had, of course, been responsible for two excruciatingly bad movies and had, according to the media, sold out his talents for the almighty dollar; but she couldn't tell Brent that.

The boy huddled into the corner of the seat as far from her as he could get. 'Will you stay?' he muttered.

With a pang of helpless guilt she said, 'No, I can't, Brent. I'm going straight back to San Francisco.'

He turned his face away from her to stare out of the window, but not before she saw a couple of tears trickle down his cheeks. Feeling absolutely rotten, for this was the first time the boy had given any indication that he had even noticed her presence, Paige accelerated down the hill. She had to go back to San Francisco. She wanted to spend the next two weeks in her apartment, getting her life in some sort of order. She couldn't stay in some God-forsaken spot in the middle of nowhere just because a little boy shed a few tears.

None of which alleviated the fact that she felt like a skunk. Or some other very low form of life. Had she needed to make it so horribly clear to Brent that she was simply a courier taking him from point 'a' to point 'b' and depositing him like a parcel of goods?

She drove into the village. Under other conditions the little array of shops would have enchanted her, for they looked so like the set for an old Western movie that she almost expected Clint Eastwood to gallop round the restaurant twirling a lariat. She pulled up beside the petrol station. 'Leave your bag on the seat, Brent, and we'll go inside to find out where your father lives.'

She'd look a fool if he wasn't home, she thought in sudden panic, wishing now that she had taken the precaution of phoning; although the law firm had sent Travis Renshaw a registered letter about his son's arrival, there had not been the time for a reply, and in Whitehorse she had been too rushed to bother with a telephone call.

She and Brent walked across the gravel, the boy sulkily trailing behind. The air was cool, but clean and crisp in a way it never was in San Francisco. Paige took a deep breath and pushed open the door to the station.

The hinges creaked. Enter the heroine, thought Paige,

and ushered Brent in ahead of her.

The room's sole occupant said, 'Howdy.'

'Hello,' Paige responded, trying hard not to stare. This man, even in his heyday, had never been as good-looking as Clint Eastwood, and his heyday was a long time past. No self-respecting laundrywoman would have touched his clothes: the patched black trousers, the red-checked shirt beneath which long underwear coyly peeked, the disgraceful old stetson. His beard hid most of his face. But through its undergrowth he appeared to be smiling.

She smiled back and said, 'We're looking for Travis Renshaw. Please can you tell me where he lives?'

'Sure thing. Midway 'twixt Teko Bay and Laird's Inlet, that's where Travis hangs his hat.' With the accuracy of practice, the old man spat into a tin he was holding in his right hand.

Paige dragged her eyes back to his face. The names meant nothing to her. 'I'm a stranger here,' she said politely. 'Do I go right or left at the crossroads?'

The old man cackled. 'You'll be drivin' forever if you try to find him that way.'

She felt Brent creep a little closer to her. 'So how do I find him?'

'Your best bet is to go next door to the restaurant. Likely Dick'd take you over.'

With a sinking sensation in the pit of her stomach, Paige said, 'Over where?'

He spat again, taking his time. 'Over the lake,' he replied, grinning maliciously. 'He lives on t'other side of Lake Tahini.'

Conscious of a strong desire to wipe the smirk from his face, Paige said coldly, 'Thank you so much. Come along, Brent.'

'What's he eating?' Brent demanded.

'Chewin' tabaccy,' the old man answered, winking at

the boy. 'Ain't you never tried it, son? You got a treat in store.'

Paige had had enough of him. She pulled Brent out of the petrol station and stalked across the gravel to the restaurant, which a sign announced as The Cosy Corner. It was certainly warm inside, and smelled heavily of hot fat. A battery of eyes swung round as she entered. She said composedly, 'Is Dick here, please?'

A rangy young man sitting in front of a plateful of chips and hamburger said agreeably, 'That's me.'

Encouraged, Paige said in a rush, 'We're looking for Travis Renshaw. I understand he lives across the lake and that you might take us there.'

'Sure thing,' he drawled. 'You in a hurry?'

She was. But in deference to the hamburger and chips she said, 'Not at all. Although I would like you to bring me right back here.' With another twinge of panic she added, 'Provided he's home, that is. He didn't say anything to you about expecting anyone?'

'Nope . . . haven't seen him for a while. But he's likely home. He's got a horse to feed.'

At any other time the logic of this statement would have amused Paige. Dick was now dousing the chips with ketchup. She said to Brent, 'Why don't we order something? That way your father won't have to worry about feeding us as soon as we get there.'

'Can I have the same as him?'

'You can have whatever you like,' she answered recklessly. Brent's foreboding seemed to be transferring itself to her. Perhaps she was just hungry, she thought, steering the little boy towards a booth. Travis Renshaw wasn't an ogre, even if he did live on the wrong side of the lake. He must be a decent man, or Stephanie Renshaw would not have entrusted their son to his care. Would she?

Paige buried her nose in the menu, remembering the little that Barbara had been able to tell her about Brent's mother. 'No real harm in her,' Barb had said with legal objectivity. 'And certainly not mercenary; she never attempted to get her hands on a penny of her husband's money. Nor did she attempt to divorce him. Funny, really. She just went from lover to lover and country to country, and as far as I can tell her only criterion for a lover—apart from good looks, wealth and a penchant for the fast lane—was that he accept her son along with her. I suppose in her own way she wasn't a terribly bad mother.'

'Not a terribly good one, either,' Paige had responded unsympathetically.'

'Well, her sins, if such they were, caught up with her. She drowned in a swimming pool in Beverly Hills in front of several witnesses who were apparently too drunk to go to her aid. Strange, isn't it, that she ended up in the town her husband had fled from in disgrace only three years before . . .'

'Ready to order?'

Paige came back to the present with a start, ordering a hamburger and chips for Brent and a hot turkey sandwich for herself. The waitress, a handsome, big-busted girl, was the only other female in this room full of men. Frontier country, thought Paige wryly, wondering what had brought Brent's father here, for according to Barbara Travis Renshaw had been as at home in the fast lane as his former wife. Nelson's Landing was not the fast lane. Teko Bay, across that vast stretch of water, was surely even less so.

But Travis Renshaw's choice of residence was no concern of hers, she reminded herself hurriedly. She would leave Brent with his father and come right back with Dick, and tomorrow Barbara would get an earful about the laxity of the arrangements of her law firm. At least the village was far enough north that daylight lasted well into the evening; she was thankful for that.

The hot turkey sandwich was extremely good, and Paige's spirits rose as she ate. Brent looked happier too. By the time they had finished, Dick had demolished a huge piece of cream pie and two cups of coffee. He waved his paper napkin at them. 'Ready?'

Once they were outside, she introduced herself to Dick and explained that Brent was Travis Renshaw's son. Dick scratched his head dubiously. 'Never heard he had a son. He never said nuthin' about it to me.'

'I assure you he does,' Paige said crisply, by now sensitive enough to Brent to feel the child's inner shrinking. 'How long does it take to go across the lake? It'll be a real adventure, won't it, Brent?'

'Half an hour. We might as well go. You never know when the wind'll come up.'

Paige parked the car by the dock where three seaplanes swayed at their moorings, and handed Brent's luggage to Dick. Then she helped Brent into the aluminium boat and climbed in herself. After tossing a couple of life-jackets at them, Dick hauled an old army blanket from under the thwarts. 'Gonna be cold,' he yelled above the sputter of the outboard motor.

In a swirl of wake they drew away from the dock, and Dick opened the engine to full power. Conversation was impossible. Paige sat quietly, her arm around Brent's shoulders to protect him from the wind. The boat's prow slapped against the water. The mountains surrounded her, enclosing her in a world of stark and primitive beauty; the snow on their flanks was now tinged with pink, while the glacier at the far end of the lake was shrouded in shadow. The wind sliced through her thin summer clothes like a hunting knife, sharp and cold. She was suddenly exhilarated, lifted out of herself to become part of the arc of sky and the grandeur of mountain, her breath the voice of the wind.

For Paige, the journey was over too soon. Dick had crossed the lake at an angle, then followed the shore to a cove sheltered by a headland, where a weathered log wharf reached out from the sand like a skeletal finger. He turned off the motor, and into the ringing silence said, 'That's mighty odd.'

The mountains were out of sight, hidden by the ranks of spruce and fir. Paige said, 'What's odd?'

'His boat's not here. He always moors it here, even when you can navigate the river.'

Her exhilaration vanished. 'Do you mean *he* isn't here?'

'Kinda looks that way. He ain't in town, his boat wasn't at the dock there.' With swift expertise, Dick lashed the prow of the boat to the wharf. 'Well, he can't be far. Must have gone up the inlet. You get out first, ma'am, and I'll hand the little guy up.'

The silence beat against Paige's ears. No wind, no waves, no bird calls. Just a dead, aching silence that was a presence in itself. She clambered out of the boat, almost glad to hear the scrape of her shoe against the wooden boards of the dock. She took Brent's two bags from Dick, then stretched out her hand to help the boy up on the wharf; his outfit looked even more incongruous than it had in Whitehorse, and his hand stayed clasped in hers.

Dick said casually, 'Travis's place is 'bout half a mile up the trail, you can't miss it. He's gotta be back by mornin', on account of the horse.'

He had been untying the hawser as he spoke. 'You're not leaving?' Paige squeaked.

'Plannin' on it,' he said in faint surprise.

'But you can't——'

He gave the sky an expert glance. 'It'll be dark in an hour and I got things to do back home—I can't hang around. You ain't got a worry in the world, ma'am; the person's not born who could get lost between Teko Bay and Laird's Inlet.'

'But how will I get back?'

Dick tossed the rope under the prow. 'Likely Travis'll bring you back tomorrow. Weather report's OK for the next couple of days.' He touched his hand to his hat brim and crouched to start the motor.

Fighting the mad urge to throw Brent and his luggage back into the boat and to jump in after them, Paige said faintly, 'You must let me pay you for the fuel.'

Her voice was drowned out in the snarl of the engine. 'No need,' Dick shouted. 'Travis'll settle up when I see him.'

The boat swirled in a semicircle and headed across the lake, Dick hunched over the tiller. The wake rippled into shore, breaking into tiny waves on the sand. Then, as the boat disappeared from sight around the headland, the echo of the motor was swallowed up by the silence.

Paige stood still, Brent's fingers curled within her own. She was extremely glad of his company, for the utter quiet was disconcerting; San Francisco was never this quiet. 'Well,' she said, 'another adventure,' and was relieved to hear that her voice sounded almost normal. 'I guess we'd better start walking, buddy. Can you carry the small bag if I carry the big one?'

'What'll we do if he's not there?' Brent asked in a small voice.

'We'll just settle in and make ourselves at home and wait for him,' Paige said with far more confidence than she was feeling. How could Brent's father have put them in such a position? He had known they were coming. He could at least have had the decency to be home when they arrived.

'Let's go!' she said.

There was only one way to go. The track was wide and grassy, not at all Paige's conception of a wilderness trail. But she was not about to complain, for she was wearing low-heeled pumps more suited to city pavements than to the woods, and Brent's footwear was equally unsuitable. They trudged along, by unspoken consent still hand in hand. In some places the feathery branches of pine trees overhung the path, and the scent of their needles saturated the air. Although the woods were shadowed and still, the silence was now broken by the whine of mosquitoes.

Unconsciously Paige was hurrying, wanting to reach their destination before dark. Her uneasiness had increased to an atavistic prickling on the back of her neck; she had to fight the urge to keep looking back over her shoulder. Brent's short legs scurried along beside her, and she felt a rush of protectiveness towards him, coupled with a strong desire to throw every swear word she knew—and because of the nature of her work she knew a few—in the face of Travis Renshaw.

If she ever came face to face with him.

She pushed this thought away. 'Do you know what I need, Brent? Twelve hours' sleep in a comfortable bed. I feel as though we left San Francisco three days ago, don't you?'

'When are we going to get there?' said Brent.

'Soon. Dick said it was only half a mile.'

Brent stopped dead in his tracks. 'What's that noise?' he asked, his violet eyes wide.

'I don't hear——'

Then she heard it, a rustling in the trees. 'I expect it's a squirrel,' she began. But the noise was louder now, far too loud for a squirrel. Over the rhythm of running feet, a high-pitched baying split the air.

Her hair stood up on end. She dropped the case she was carrying, grabbed Brent and hoisted him over her shoulder. Two black shadows emerged from the trees.

Wolves.

Paige kicked the bag so it made a barrier between her and the animals, and said in the voice she had used when Pedro had been caught shoplifting, 'Go away! Get lost! I'm bigger than you are.'

The animals trotted out into the track and sat down, pink tongues lolling, big jaws laughing.

They were dogs.

Not wolves.

Paige let out her pent-up breath in a shaky sigh and said, 'It's all right, Brent. You can stop choking me. They must be your father's dogs, which means we must be nearly there.'

The little boy loosened his stranglehold on Paige's neck and peered cautiously over his shoulder. 'They're big,' he said.

Paige was in complete agreement. What was Travis Renshaw afraid of? she thought irascibly. That someone might steal him?

They were huskies, one black and tan, the other brindled. 'Nice dogs,' she said sycophantically. 'Is your master home?' The brindled one sidled closer, sniffing Paige's shoe. As she bent and patted its head, it stood there with an idiotic grin on its face. 'I think they're friendly, Brent,' she said drily. 'Let's keep walking, OK?'

When she put Brent on the ground, the brindled dog licked him on the chin. For a moment it looked as though the boy was going to retreat. Then he smiled uncertainly. 'He's as big as me.'

'We'll have to ask your father what his name is.'

The smile disappeared. 'Are we nearly there?'

A few minutes later the trail opened into a clearing where a log cabin and several outbuildings were scattered among the tall trees; beyond them, in the dusk, Paige could see a fenced garden and a horse grazing in the paddock. In a spectacular backdrop, the mountains clawed their way into the sky.

How incredibly beautiful, thought Paige.

'Nobody's home,' said Brent.

She dragged her mind back to practicalities. He was right. The windows of the cabin were dark.

In San Francisco, Paige would not have contemplated entering a stranger's deserted house. But the rules were different here, she knew that already. 'Let's go inside and find that bed . . . I'm so glad we ate before we came.'

The cabin door moved smoothly on oiled hinges. The porch was aggressively tidy, jackets hung on hooks, snowshoes and skis on brackets on the wall, boots lined up on the floor. From the size of the boots, Travis Renshaw was a big man, Paige thought, and felt again that qualm of unease. She pushed open the door of the cabin proper.

The main room was spacious, with a stove against the front wall, and a couch and two comfortable armchairs in front of the picture windows that overlooked the mountains; to her left was the kitchen, to her right three steps to what she presumed was the sleeping area. Although she knew the place was empty, she called conventionally, 'Hello! Anyone home?' Then, from long habit, she fumbled for the light switch.

Smart move, Paige, she berated herself. You're in the backwoods now, remember? An oil lamp which she had no idea how to use was standing on a pine table by the window. 'I guess we'll have to go to bed, Brent,' she said. 'No choice. She led the way up the stairs. There was only one bedroom, with a double bed covered by a duvet.

Travis Renshaw had not even bothered to set up a bed for his son. So we'll sleep in your bed, Mr Renshaw, she thought vengefully. And if you happen to come home in the middle of the night, you can damn well sleep on the floor.

'I'll fetch your case and you can change into your pyjamas,' she said cheerfully to Brent. 'Hope you don't mind sharing a bed with me.'

Getting Brent ready for bed involved finding the outside toilet, patting the dogs, wrestling with the pump at the kitchen sink, washing in ice-cold water, and tripping up the stairs in the dark. Brent was not downright disobedient, but neither was he co-operative; Paige's patience was worn thin by the time she finally pulled the duvet up to his chin. 'Goodnight,' she said, perhaps a little more sharply than she had intended.

Even in the gloom she could see his big eyes watching her unwaveringly. 'You going away now?' he quavered.

Her heart melted. Brent must be used to being left alone, for Stephanie Renshaw would surely not have stayed home once he had been put to bed. She sat down on the duvet. 'Do you know what I'm going to do? Once I've washed my face I'm going to crawl into bed beside you and go right to sleep. And I promise I'll still be here in the morning when you wake up. OK?'

'OK.'

It was not an overly enthusiastic response, but Paige sensed that he believed her. She threaded her way through the unfamiliar furniture to the kitchen, shuddered as the cold water trickled down her neck, used Brent's toothbrush, and made her way back to the bedroom. She did not have any pyjamas. She did not even have a change of clothes. So she took off her blue cotton trousers and overblouse, laid them on the chair, and got into bed wearing her camisole and briefs. The sheets were cold. Shivering, she murmured, 'Goodnight, Brent.'

'G'night,' he whispered.

She lay quietly until the duvet had hoarded her bodyheat and warmed her. By then, Brent was asleep. She had promised him she would go straight to sleep herself. But, although her body was tired, her brain could not rest, and her nerves were on edge for the sound of Travis Renshaw's return.

Poor Brent. He was not a particularly likeable child, but then, what chance had he had? His mother was a fortune-hunter. Or a nymphomaniac, depending on how uncharitable you were. And his father, plainly, was a hermit who was not interested enough in his son's arrival to make even the slightest of preparations. Not that it was any of her business, she told herself hastily.

However, as she lay there in the dark, Paige discovered it was not as easy to say that as it had been early this morning. Somehow, through a day of mishaps and contretemps, Brent's fate had become important to her. Important enough that she was angry about his father's absence, and worried about the kind of life a small boy would lead so far from civilisation.

It was none of her business, she told herself again. By this time tomorrow she would be home in her apartment, beginning her vacation.

In an effort to shut out the press of silence from her ears, she closed her eyes and imagined that she was in her apartment in Marco Towers, with the hum of traffic and the shouts of street hawkers drifting up the three floors . . . on warm evenings she could hear jazz from the bars near the corner, the muted blare of trumpets and the croon of saxophones . . .

CHAPTER TWO

A BRILLIANT white light was shining right in Paige's face. For a split second the light filled her with terror. Her apartment had been broken into, she thought wildly. But as she sat up, shielding her eyes with one hand, sanity returned and she croaked, 'Turn it off!'

'Just who the devil are you?'

The voice was unmistakably masculine. Paige squinted against the light, but the source of the voice was invisible to her. 'For goodness' sake, turn it off,' she demanded more strongly, memory rushing back. 'You know perfectly well who we are.'

'*We?*'

Mercifully the light moved away from her. Her vision blurred by concentric circles of throbbing colour, Paige hissed, 'Don't you dare wake him up! You're not *that* interested in meeting him, or you'd have been home.'

Her reward was to have the light trained on her face again. She scrunched up her eyes and heard the voice say, 'Young lady, I have no idea who you are or who the child is who's lucky enough to be sharing the bed with you. My bed, I might add——'

'Then you should have made one for him,' she interrupted rudely. 'And keep your voice down, he's worn out and needs his sleep.'

'So do I.' The voice was now dangerously quiet.

She remembered her earlier vow. 'Then sleep on the floor,' she suggested sweetly, and flopped back on the pillow.

A hand reached out from the darkness and seized her shoulder. 'This is ridiculous!' the man rasped. 'You have two choices. You can either get up and give me an explanation—and it had better be good—or else I'll take my clothes off and join you. It's bloody cold out here, and as I believe I may have mentioned, it is my bed.'

Paige sat up in a hurry, her breasts bouncing under the thin satin camisole. 'You will not!' she announced, forgetting to keep her voice down. Beside her Brent stirred restlessly. She put her hand on the mound of his body under the duvet and said softly, 'Shh, love, go back to sleep.'

For a moment the light wavered. It was powerful enough to have reduced her features to the essential elegance of a bone structure that was perfectly proportioned; her firm chin, delightfully straight nose, sweep of cheekbone and brow were clearly delineated, as was the cap of short-cropped hair that emphasised her long slender neck and wide-spaced eyes. The camisole, of palest blue, bared the creamy shoulders and the shadowed valley between her breasts, while her wrists and hands had the delicate bones of a wild bird.

Abruptly the light shifted to the floor by the bed. 'Your last chance,' said the man.

Quite suddenly it occurred to Paige that she might have made a terrible mistake, that she and Brent might be in the wrong house. After all, there had been no indication that the log cabin belonged to Travis Renshaw. She had simply assumed that it had. Which would, she thought with disproportionate relief, explain why there had been no bed for Brent. She said with quick warmth, '*Please* put the light out—I think I may have made a dreadful mistake. Tell me—what's your name?'

The light remained on. 'Travis Renshaw,' said the man. 'What's yours? If we're all going to share the bed, we should at least introduce ourselves.'

'You're really Travis Renshaw? Oh, dear,' said Paige in dismay.

'I didn't think I was that repulsive,' he replied, sounding genuinely amused.

He had a very attractive voice, deep and resonant, which amusement made all the more attractive. Thoroughly confused, Paige blurted, 'As you've totally blinded me with that flashlight, how should I know if you're repulsive or not?'

'Good point.' Obligingly he put the torch behind his back, whereupon that the light became diffuse enough for Paige to discover that he was actually sitting on the bed. 'What's the verdict?' he asked.

The voice seemed to have cast a spell on her. Paige stared at the man's face. His hair was blacker than the darkness, his brows black slashes, his eyes impenetrable shadows. A man of the night, she thought with an inward shiver, seeing the lines in his cheeks, the sculpted line of his mouth, the strong line of his jaw. His shoulders, in silhouette, were broad and solid, the rest of his body a dark mass. This was the man whose son she had travelled hundreds of miles to deliver; this was the man she had blithely told to sleep on the floor.

Gathering her scattered wits, she said firmly, 'If you wouldn't mind leaving the room, I'll get dressed and we can continue this conversation in the living-room.'

'Ah, but I would mind. I wouldn't want you to fall and hurt yourself in the dark.'

While Paige's hair was not as red as Barbara's, it was still red. 'Fine,' she said briskly, swung her legs over the side of the bed and stood up.

'Better and better,' Travis Renshaw said, unabashedly allowing the flashlight to travel the slender length of her body.

Just wait till I get you downstairs! I'll tell you a thing or two, she raged inwardly. Flouncing past him, she struggled into her trousers and top. The floorboards were cold under her feet, and the chill air brought goose-bumps to her arms. 'Please lead the way,' she said, with all the dignity she could muster.

He got up from the bed, taking his time, and walked towards her; he was considerably taller than her five feet seven. Stopping a few inches away from her, the flashlight now directed at their feet, he said, 'Didn't your mother ever tell you not to get into a stranger's bed? Particularly the bed of a man who's been living in the wilderness for over three years. There's a decided dearth of women up here, you know.' His hand drifted up to brush her cheek 'Especially beautiful young women like you.'

Something inside her seemed to be melting. Something that had been frozen for months. But Paige was fully dressed now, and if she had learned one thing in her job it was how to preserve outward appearances, no matter what she was feeling inside. She looked him full in the eye. 'Had you prepared for us, we wouldn't have been in your bed. But thank you for the compliment, anyway.' She smiled, indicating the stairs. 'After you.'

His brows knit. 'You're a cool customer, Mrs Whoever-You-Are. I think you're right. It's time for explanations.'

He drew the bedroom door shut behind them, put the flashlight on the table and lit the oil lamp, turning down the wick so that the light was a soft glow. Then he filled a kettle at the sink, put it on the propane stove, and got out mugs and a teapot. Paige, looking more composed than she felt, curled up in one of the armchairs, tucking her feet under her. She could see stars sprinkling the sky, and below them the bulk of the mountains. She had no idea what the time was.

A few minutes later Travis Renshaw carried in a tray, passing her a mug of tea, the milk and sugar, and a plate of muffins. She helped herself. 'Thank you.'

He sat down across from her. 'OK—who are you, who is the child, and why are you here?'

She remembered Brent saying, 'I don't have a father,' and felt anger as scaldingly hot as the tea. 'Why don't we drop the charades, Mr Renshaw? You know who Brent is, and you knew someone was bringing him here.'

There was no amusement in his voice now. 'I asked you your name.'

'Paige Montgomery. Miss. From San Francisco. The boy is, of course, your son.'

His mug crashed down on the table. 'I don't know what your game is, Miss Montgomery, but I don't find this the slightest bit funny.'

She said as slowly as if she were explaining something to an idiot, 'The child in the bedroom is your son—Eustace Percival Brent Renshaw, to give him his full name. Some time during the last week you received a letter from the law firm of Deschamps, Filbert and Young in San Francisco to the effect that your late wife has left the boy in your care. I was the one chosen to bring him up here.'

Travis Renshaw sat up as if turned to stone; Paige could not even hear the sound of his breathing. He was silent for what must have been two full minutes. Then he said, each word as cutting as a shard of ice, 'I do not have a son.'

Whatever Paige had expected, it had not been flat denial. She retorted, 'Your wife seemed to be under the impression that you did—in her will she left her son in your guardianship.'

'You finally got something right. *Her* son. Her son, Miss Montgomery. Not mine.'

'Brent is five years old. You were living with her then—he has to be your son.'

'Don't be naïve!'

She flinched at the savagery in his tone. 'Then whose son is he?'

He got up from the chair and faced the window, his back rigid. 'Five and a half years ago my wife left me for another man. Before she left, she informed me categorically that the child she was bearing was her lover's child. Not mine.'

Paige must have made a tiny choked sound, because he suddenly swivelled, his hands clenched at his sides. 'And spare me your sympathy, for God's sake.'

It was her turn to sit in silence. Then she slowly got to her feet. 'I would have to be both naïve and a fool to offer you unwanted sympathy, Mr Renshaw, and I am neither. I'm simply the conveyor of a very small boy from the hotel where he was staying in San Francisco to your place of residence . . . Those were my instructions, and that's what I have done.'

'Then first thing tomorrow morning, Miss Montgomery, you may undo your instructions and take him straight back to San Francisco.'

'I can't do that!'

'You not only can, you will.'

She took a deep, steadying breath, trying to think. 'First of all, did you get the lawyer's letter?'

'No. I haven't been to the mainland for over a week.'

'But it was registered!'

'This is Teko Bay,' he said testily. 'The tremendous sense of urgency that seems to motivate the rest of the world doesn't always operate here.'

'More's the pity.' But then the implications of what he had said struck her. She bit her lip. 'So I'm the one who brought you the news of your wife's death. I'm sorry.'

'I have already requested that you spare me your sympathy.'

Paige stared at him, noticing for the first time that his eyes were blue. Not the violet-blue of Brent's, but steel-blue. Lake Tahini would be that colour under a summer sky, she thought intuitively: hinting at unknown depths, reflecting rather than revealing. Ice-cold, as this man seemed to be.

Deciding to go on the attack, she said, 'I cannot take the boy back.'

'You will take the boy back.'

'I cannot.' She stepped closer to him, refusing to be intimidated. 'He has nowhere to go and no one else to take him.' For a moment her indignation flared. 'When I picked him up at six o'clock this morning he was in the care of a maid who couldn't wait to get rid of him and who looked as if she hated little boys. His mother is dead. He has no brothers or sisters. I don't know if he's your son or not. But you were legally married to his mother at the time of her death—you *have* to take him!'

'Since you seem so upset by his plight,' Travis Renshaw sneered, 'why don't you take him? After all, how do I know this isn't some kind of a set-up? Maybe he's your child and you're just trying to get rid of him.'

Deliberately Paige allowed the contempt she was feeling to show in her face. 'Are you as inhuman as you appear?' she snapped. 'I find it difficult to believe that you are.'

'I will not allow you or anyone else to foist Stephanie's bastard on me,' he grated. 'That boy is the son of her first lover. First official lover, that is,' he added cynically. 'I don't want anything to do with him. Do I make myself clear?'

'You make a great many things clear,' she blazed. 'Your selfishness. Your insensitivity. Your inability to forgive. I begin to understand why Stephanie needed a lover.'

She heard his breath hiss between his teeth. 'Oh, do you, Miss Montgomery? What a clever creature you are! But are you clever enough to understand that *I* could do with a lover right now? Three years is a long time to go without a woman.'

At some point in this nasty little speech he had taken her by the shoulders. She could feel the dig of his fingers in her flesh, and for the second time since she had landed at Teko Bay she was afraid. A different type of wolf, she thought with a touch of hysteria. Happy vacation, Paige. 'Let go,' she said, and was ashamed to hear her voice shake.

'Not yet.' He moved one hand to clasp her chin, then bent his head and kissed her.

Paige knew enough about the seamy side of city life to have read rape reports, and consequently to have at least secondhand knowledge of the degradation involved. She felt something of that degradation now, for this was not a kiss with any tenderness, any sense of mutual exploration or pleasure; rather it was an expression of power, of an anger she did not deserve, of a frustration that was none of her business. Deliberately she allowed her body to sway against his, buried her free hand in his hair as if to caress it, took hold of a good handful, and pulled as hard as she could.

He released her so abruptly that she staggered, his obscenity one Pedro would have admired. She braced herself for whatever he might do next, knowing that if he touched her again she would scream the house down.

He dropped his hands to his sides, stepped away from her and said very formally, 'I apologise, Miss Montgomery. I had no right to do that.'

Paige sat down hard in the nearest chair, partly from

sheer surprise, partly because her legs seemed disinclined
to hold her up. 'You're also incomprehensible,' she said
weakly. 'Add that to the list.'

'Look, I've had enough of this. Go back to bed, and I'll
take both of you across the lake tomorrow morning.'

She dredged up the last of her energy. 'No, Mr
Renshaw,' she said quietly. 'I have reservations for only
one person from Whitehorse to San Francisco tomorrow.
And I'm the one who will be using them. Brent stays here
with you.'

'The boy goes back to San Francisco,' he said
implacably. 'If all else fails, I'm physically stronger than
the two of you put together. Goodnight, Miss
Montgomery.'

Menace underlay the evenly spoken words, and Paige
seemed to have run out of arguments. She frowned at
him, feeling like a very small wave trying to erode the base
of a granite cliff. There must be a crack in the cliff, or a
weak point she could attack. But she had no idea where it
was. It was time to retreat, to regroup her forces, she
thought, unsurprised by the military flavour of her
metaphors. For this was war, and Travis Renshaw the
enemy.

Holding her head high, she crossed the room and
climbed the stairs to the bedroom. She closed the door
behind her, leaning against the panels, and not until then
did she begin to tremble. The man was an elemental
force, like the wind and the waves. Immovable as the
mountains. Cold as the lake. She had no doubt of his
physical strength and of the threat it implied. While the
vision this conjured up had elements of the comic, she
knew there was nothing comical about her situation.

Travis Renshaw refused to acknowledge Brent as his
son and refused to provide a home for the boy. What was
she to do?

What on earth was she to do?

Someone was tugging at her hair. A small voice said, 'You awake?'

Paige struggled against the weight of sleep, a weight which was smothering her and under which she wanted to remain buried, supine, dead to the world. It was too early to wake up. She wanted to sleep longer. She wanted to sleep forever . . .

'Wake up!'

The thin edge of panic in Brent's request sliced through the fog in her brain. She opened her eyes, rubbing at them and yawning. 'Hello, Brent,' she mumbled. 'Ouch! Don't pull my hair like that.'

'I want my breakfast.'

'Please, Paige,' she said, rather spoiling the effect with another huge yawn.

'Is he here? Did he come back?'

Paige burrowed her head in the pillow, not needing to ask to whom the pronoun referred. 'Oh, yes, he came back.'

'Is he here now?'

She pricked her ears. There wasn't a sound from the rest of the cabin, and she had the feeling dawn was long gone. 'I'm sure he's around somewhere,' she said. She should have said 'your father', not 'he'; but last night Travis Renshaw had refused that role.

Nevertheless, she seemed to have made a decision while she slept; she was leaving Teko Bay today and she was not taking Brent with her. Her arrival had been a shock to Travis, the news of his wife's death and the unexpected appearance of a son a far greater shock. But by now he would have had time to think, to realise that he had spoken too hastily last night; in the sober light of morning he would realise that he had to offer Stephanie's child a home. Common decency would demand it, if nothing else. And he and Brent would work out their joint destiny far better if she were absent. So she assured herself, ignoring the nibble of conscience. Her decision might seem cold-blooded, but it was necessary.

She would have given all the money in her bank account to have been able to pull the duvet over her head and go back to sleep. But she knew Brent well enough to know that he would persist with his questions until she got up. 'Why don't you fetch your clothes and I'll help you get dressed?' she said in resignation.

Brent scrambled off the bed, gathered up the clothes he had worn yesterday, and threw them and himself up on the bed, one foot nearly landing in Paige's face. She said with casual interest, 'Did you break your little toe once, Brent?' It was bent inwards at an awkward angle.

'Nope. Th'other one's the same,' he said, and obligingly stuck out his left foot, struggling with the buttons on his shirt at the same time. 'My mother said I was born like that.'

He was so palpably unconcerned that Paige had no wish to dwell on what was only the most minor of defects. 'Here, let me help you,' she said. 'Then we'll go and find your father.' There. She had said the word. Because Travis Renshaw had to be Brent's father.

Ten minutes later they pushed open the front door of the cabin, for, by an unspoken agreement, finding its owner seemed to have taken precedence over breakfast. The sun was shining. Birds were singing in the trees. As the two dogs came gambolling across the grass to greet them, Brent gave the nearest thing to a laugh that Paige had heard, and cautiously began patting the black and tan one on the nose; it wagged its tail, snuffling into his palm. Paige moved out into the sunlight, lifting her face to its warmth. It gleamed in her russet hair and faithfully outlined the hollows beneath her cheekbones and the faint blue shadows under her eyes.

For a moment she forgot all her concerns in the simple pleasure of the fragrant pines and the unclouded sky.

'Good morning.'

Her head jerked sideways. Travis Renshaw was standing watching her from the shadow of a giant old oak that marked the edge of the trail. Slowly she walked towards him as he too stepped out into the sun.

His hair was black as the raven's wing is black, iridescent in the light. His eyes held all the brilliance of the sky. He was, Paige decided, the most attractive man she had ever seen. Yet his features were guarded, and his conventional words of greeting had held no real warmth.

'Is it still morning?' she asked lightly. 'I wondered if we'd slept past noon.'

'Ten-thirty.'

She was about to make some trivial rejoinder when she saw him glance over her shoulder and freeze to stillness, like a buck at the scent of danger. She followed his gaze. Brent had chased the other dog into the sunshine and was hugging it, his tumbled brown curls buried in the dog's neck. Then the boy raised his head; his eyes were the deep purple of delphiniums.

'Stephanie's eyes,' the man said hoarsely, as if the words were being torn from his throat. 'My God . . . Stephanie.'

Paige stared at him and felt her heart contract, for she had never heard such agony in a man's voice before. Instinctively she circled his wrist with her fingers.

He jerked his arm free. 'You're leaving here today and you're taking that boy with you,' he said in a savage undertone. 'I won't have him here.'

Although Brent could not have heard him, there was anger in every line of the man's body, and repudiation in the blazing eyes. The little boy shrank back, his chubby fist clenched in the brindled dog's ruff.

'You can't *do* that!' Paige whispered, distraught.

'I'll do what I damn well please.'

It was a declaration of war. 'Then you'll have to carry us bodily,' Paige said. 'You haven't heard how loudly I can scream, have you, Mr Renshaw? I'll make you the laughing-stock of Nelson's Landing.'

'You little——'

In ludicrous anticlimax, a voice wafted through the trees. 'Hello there!'

Paige looked up. A man, thin, bearded, was waving at them from the trail. 'Who's that?' she said blankly. Teko Bay was the last place she would have expected visitors.

'A neighbour,' Travis said furiously. 'Wait here.'

He strode up the slope. But Paige needed an ally, and something in the demeanour of the other man gave her hope. She hurried up the slope towards him. He tipped his hat to her and said with a courtesy that Travis Renshaw could well have emulated, 'Good morning.'

She gave him her most generous smile and said, 'Good morning. I'm Paige Montgomery.'

'Felix Cameron.' He had a firm handshake and showed no surprise at finding a woman at his neighbour's cabin at ten-thirty in the morning. His brown hair was curly and too long, but very clean, while his grave grey eyes regarded the world behind gold-rimmed glasses. Paige trusted him instantly.

Determined to keep the initiative, she said limpidly, 'I'm from San Francisco. I brought Mr Renshaw's son here yesterday.'

Travis said with the quietness of extreme rage, 'The boy is not my son.'

She glanced over at him. The jut of his jaw and his wide-legged stance were strangely familiar to her; she remembered Brent glowering at her in defiance beside the car in Nelson's Landing and knew in a flash of intuition that Travis Renshaw must be Brent's father. Brent might look like the dead Stephanie. But violet eyes were not the only things one could inherit.

She locked her gaze with Travis's, and said just as quietly as he, 'Brent *is* your son.'

Felix said calmly, 'I have a registered letter here for you, Travis. From San Francisco. The postmistress had left it in your box, figuring you'd be over before this. Would it have anything to do with Miss Montgomery's arrival?'

Paige would have sworn there was a twinkle in Felix's eye, and found herself wondering how often Travis Renshaw was openly defied. 'That's the letter I told you about,' she said to Travis with a deadpan expression on her face.

The look Travis gave her would have withered a lesser woman; Paige, however, was used to confronting slum landlords and fierce Puerto Rican mothers, and returned it levelly. *Courage,* she thought, knowing he wouldn't do anything with Felix there.

Travis ripped the letter open and read it in a scowling silence. Then he said with barely suppressed sarcasm, 'Perhaps you're not aware of the exact wording of the will, Miss Montgomery. "I leave my son, Eustace Percival Brent Renshaw, to the legal guardianship of my husband, Travis Brent Renshaw." It does not say the boy is *my* son. And as I thought I had made clear to you last night, I will not accept Stephanie's bastard into my home. So why don't you go down to the cabin and pack your things, and I'll take the two of you back to the village?'

Brent *was* his son; she knew it in her bones. Paige stood still, her brain racing. She could not possibly leave with Brent, for that would deprive the boy of his only living relative. 'I have a better suggestion,' she said coldly. 'Perhaps Felix would take me over to the village.'

'You're not leaving without the boy.'

'Then I'll swim across the lake.'

He gave her a thoroughly unpleasant smile. 'Do that—

you'll die of hypothermia in twenty minutes.'

'You're putting me in an impossible situation!'

'No, Miss Montgomery—you've put yourself in this situation.'

Ignoring him, she stormed, 'I can't leave with Brent—he has nowhere else to go. And I can't stay, either. I have a plane to catch. I have a job in San Francisco. I have a life of my own, Mr Renshaw, which does not include you or Brent. You *must* provide a home for him.'

'I will not.'

'Then I'm staying,' she heard herself say. 'With Brent.'

He grasped her by the elbow. 'I don't want you here!'

'I don't want to be here!' Paige shook herself free, her cheeks scarlet with an anger that was directed as much at herself as at him. 'But what choice do I have? I can't take him back to San Francisco and dump him in the doorway of a hotel. And I certainly can't abandon him to your tender mercies—what kind of a person would that make me? You're stuck with me, Mr Renshaw. You're stuck with both of us.'

Felix cleared his throat. Paige jumped, for she had forgotten him; he had had no part in this battle of wills. Travis said tightly, 'Then you'd better stay out of my way. You and the boy.'

He wheeled and loped down the hill towards the cabin. Brent and the brindled dog were in his path. Brent said in a small, clear voice that carried all the way up the slope, 'I don't like you.'

Travis stopped dead. Paige could only guess at the emotion in the rigid shoulders and clenched fists; she must have made an instinctive voice to follow him, because Felix took her arm and said softly, 'It's all right—he won't do anything.'

Nor did he. Turning on his heel, he vanished around the corner of the cabin.

Paige felt her knees go limp. She said in despair. '*Now* what have I done?'

Felix said easily, 'I don't know you very well, Miss Montgomery—although there's nothing like a good fight for getting to know someone—but I'd say you've remained true to your principles.'

'Call me Paige,' she said helplessly. 'It's not the first time my principles have got me in trouble. Though this seems rather more extreme than my usual messes.'

'*Is* the boy his son?'

She sighed. 'If I were asked that question in a court of law, I would have to say I don't know. Courts aren't much for feminine intuition. His wife apparently swore the child wasn't his.'

'But you don't believe her.'

'No, I don't. I'm convinced Brent is his son.'

'I see . . . He's not a bad man, Paige.'

'Tell that to his son,' she said sourly.

'We've known him for three years. He's a good neighbour, but a very private person. He's never told us anything about his marriage, for instance, and certainly nothing about a possible son. He's not what I'd call a happy man.'

'Felix,' she said in exasperation, 'it's very nice of you to make excuses for him. But here I am with only the clothes I'm standing up in, with my suitcase in a rented car on the other side of the lake and a plane waiting for me in Whitehorse.'

'You forgot the job in San Francisco.'

'Oh, I've got two weeks' leave,' she retorted. 'Two weeks to relax. Ha!'

With a sweep of his hand Felix indicated the forest and the snow-capped peaks. 'There are worse places in the world to relax.'

'You think I can relax with Travis Renshaw within ten

miles of me? Think again.'

'Interesting,' said Felix, with a gleam of humour behind his gold-rimmed glasses.

She scowled at him. 'Don't go getting any ideas—he's the most obnoxious man I've ever met, and I've met a few in my time . . . I haven't even got anything to wear if I want to wash these clothes! And Brent's stuff is only suitable for a kid in a picture-book.'

Felix said soothingly, 'You and Brent can walk home with me now, my wife Nell will give you some lunch, and this afternoon I'll go over to the village and get your bag. I can buy some jeans there for Brent—and for you too, for that matter. Or Nell, I'm sure, could lend you something to wear.'

In one speech Felix was solving all her problems—except for Travis Renshaw. Paige produced an approximation of a smile. 'We haven't had breakfast yet,' she admitted. 'That's kind of you, Felix.'

'Time someone welcomed you to Teko Bay,' he remarked with a sly smile. Raising his voice, he called, 'Brent, come along—lunch time,' then added in an aside to Paige, 'I have two daughters, seven and five. He'll be good company for them.'

A home, a wife, children and food. Paige began to feel better. She watched Brent stomp towards them and stooped so her face was level with his. 'This is Felix—we're going to his house for lunch. I'm not leaving today, Brent, I'll stay for a few days—OK?'

'I don't want to stay here. He doesn't want me.'

'He hadn't known your mother was dead. He was upset,' she replied with partial truth, infuriated to find herself now making excuses for Travis. 'It will be all right, Brent, you'll see.'

She had always despised social workers who fed children lies, and here she was doing it herself. Yet could she honestly say she would stay until Brent and Travis were reconciled? How much of your life are you willing to give up? she asked herself grimly, and got to her feet. 'If you're as hungry as I am, you're just about ready to start chomping on pine cones,' she teased.

Brent tugged at her sleeve. 'Will you still be here tomorrow?'

With a catch at her heart, she saw how afraid he was under his stolid exterior. 'I promise I will be.'

Apparently satisfied, he scratched at a mosquito bite. 'What's the dog's name?'

'Minto,' said Felix, and hoisted the boy up on his back. 'The black one's Chimo. They're huskies. Your dad has a cat as well; in fact I think she might have kittens.' He walked along briskly, showing Brent where a porcupine had eaten the bark from a tall pine tree, naming all the bird calls they heard, and interposing questions about Paige's job and yesterday's journey with further descriptions of his family. His wife, Paige heard, was a weaver who spun her own wool, and he a wildlife sculptor.

The trees thinned as the track came out on the shore of a huge body of water, where the breeze made tiny waves that sparkled in the sun and slapped against the boards of an old wharf. Felix's two-storey log house overlooked the water and the mountains beyond. 'Laird's Inlet,' Felix said. 'Pretty, eh?'

Pretty was a wholly inadequate word. Paige felt small and insignificant in the face of so much beauty; Pedro and the dingy office near Broadway could have belonged to another world, and for the first time in many weeks a feeling akin to peace visited her. If it weren't for Travis Renshaw, she thought ruefully, she would love to stay here and allow the mountains to work their magic.

Nell Cameron was a serene woman of thirty or so with clear blue eyes and a sheaf of straight blonde hair loosely braided down her back, who welcomed her visitors with unaffected pleasure. Her daughters, Fiona and Beth, were miniature replicas of herself, and before he knew it Brent had been hustled off to meet the newborn calf and the hamsters. Swiftly Felix outlined Paige's predicament. 'You must stay here with us,' Nell said warmly.

Paige would have liked nothing better but, before she could say anything, Felix said thoughtfully, 'I don't want to sound ungracious, but I'm not sure that's the best idea, Nell. If Paige and the boy stay here, Travis will never change his attitude—why should he? No, I think Paige and Brent have to spend a great deal of time right under his nose, where he can't possibly avoid them and they'll cause him maximum irritation.'

'A delightful way to spend a holiday,' Paige said with a lift of her brow. 'But much as I hate to admit it, Felix, I think you're right . . . Not that I'm convinced that anything short of a sledge-hammer will make that man change his mind.'

'He spends too much time alone,' Nell said quickly. 'You'll be good for him, Paige. And you can escape here whenever you like, our house is yours.'

Paige was touched, for in her experience simple kindness was one of the rarest of virtues. 'Thank you, Nell.'

'You look as though you need a holiday,' the other woman added shrewdly.

With Nell, Paige could be nothing but honest. 'I do, I've been working too hard. Maybe I won't have to be under his nose quite all day.'

Nell laughed. 'Home-made soup, sourdough biscuits and apple pie for lunch, and Felix will show you how the radio-phone works if you want to cancel your flight plans.'

Several hours later Paige and Brent set off for Travis's cabin, Paige carrying her small overnight case and the purchases Felix had made for them in the village. Before she left she had talked to the secretary of Deschamps, Filbert and Young, outlining the situation to her and leaving her to cancel all the reservations. Brent waved goodbye to the girls and trotted along at Paige's side, chatting about the calf, the tomcat, and the radishes he had eaten straight from the garden, in a way that warmed Paige's heart and made her all the more determined that Travis should acknowledge the boy as his son.

But as they grew closer to their destination Brent fell silent, and by the time the cabin came in sight he was dragging his feet. Paige was feeling none too happy herself. By making that one phone call she had burned her bridges, and was now committed to staying in a log cabin in the wilderness with a man who despised both her and the small boy in her care. She must be crazy, she thought unhappily. Clean out of her mind.

From behind the cabin came the snarl of a chainsaw. 'Let's go and see what he's doing,' she said.

'I want to go back to Beth's,' Brent whined, and began to cry.

Paige put down her bags and picked him up. 'Brent, listen to me,' she urged. 'The only way you'll be able to keep on playing with Beth is if your father will accept you as his son. I don't know how we're going to make him do that—but we've got to try. Both of us. We're in this together, got that? Now, let's say hello to him and then I'll put you to bed.'

Not giving him the time to protest, she put him on the ground and marched him round the corner of the cabin. Travis saw them immediately and turned off the saw, wiping the sweat from his brow. 'You came back,' he said in a non-committal voice.

'It's Brent's bedtime,' Paige said pleasantly.

'The two of you can stay in my bed. I'll sleep on the couch.'

Smile, she wanted to scream at him. It won't kill you. 'That's kind of you,' she said ironically, and turned her back on him just as he started up the chainsaw again. It could have been worse, she thought. He could have greeted them with a rifle. Or chased them with the chainsaw.

Brent fell asleep as soon as she pulled the covers over him. Paige sat by the living-room window with a book in her lap, watching the man outside as he stacked the wood he had sawn, his movements smooth and unhurried, graceful in a way that made her ache deep inside. Was he never lonely here? Did he not long for a wife and children, like Felix's, to fill his home with laughter and life? Or did he nourish himself on memories of his lost, violet-eyed Stephanie?

How was she to make him accept Brent as his son?

CHAPTER THREE

'STAY out of my way,' Travis Renshaw had said. But it was he who very thoroughly stayed out of Paige's way the next day, to the point where she was beginning to wonder if he had decided to solve the problem of her and Brent by simply vanishing into thin air. It was almost a relief, mid-afternoon, to hear him come in the back door. Brent was having a nap in the bedroom and Paige was making a sandwich for herself in the kitchen when he strode through into the living-room. He checked when he saw her. 'I thought you were outside.'

He was wearing grease-stained bush trousers and a dirty, close-fitting T-shirt, and looked both large and dangerous. 'Would you like a sandwich?' she asked politely.

'I see you're making yourself at home.'

His tone made the words a challenge. 'I didn't have much choice—you haven't exactly over-exerted yourself in the role of host.'

He walked over to the sink, peeling off his T-shirt. 'I don't want you here. I thought I'd made that clear.'

Presented with a close-up view of a naked, muscular male torso, Paige held her ground, raised her chin and said, 'Is this how you want to spend the next few days—trading insults?'

'I'd like to spend them as I spend all my days . . . in peace and quiet, in a place I chose for its solitude.' He began sluicing water over his face and hands.

The pump was noisy. Paige waited until he had finished, quelling a mad urge to lay her palm on the tanned, bare back, and then said with a valiant attempt at conciliation,

47

'I suppose we're interrupting your writing.'

He straightened, water trickling down his chest, his blue eyes glacial. 'I don't write any more.'

She was trapped in the corner with her back against the stove, and it would have taken more courage than she possessed to ask him why. 'Then I don't see why we're such a nuisance.'

Travis Renshaw reached past her for the towel. 'The boy reminds me of a time of my life I'd rather forget, and you're the most thick-skinned young woman I've ever met—most people when they know they're not welcome have the common politeness to leave.'

Colour tinged Paige's cheekbones. However, gritting her teeth, she tried once more to win him over. 'This is scarcely an average social situation,' she said. 'Have you lived alone here the last three years? If so, I can certainly understand why you'd find unexpected visitors a bit of a trial.'

'A bit of a trial?' he repeated acerbically. 'Please, Miss Montgomery, don't add stupidity to your sins.'

Her temper fraying, she grated, 'Can't we talk this whole thing over in a civilised manner?'

Taking his time, he dried his face and hands. Then he stepped closer to hang up the towel, his face only inches from hers. 'I don't feel civilised around you,' he said.

Neither did Paige around him. 'I would have thought a writer of your calibre could have come up with a more original line than that,' she said cordially.

He took her chin in his hand, his fingers touching her with a latent strength that frightened her. 'It's no line—it happens to be the truth. If you're in the habit of throwing yourself at strangers, you should learn to tell the difference.'

Paige said angrily, 'You seem to think I *want* to be here—nothing could be further from the truth. I can be out of here in five minutes once you say Brent can stay.'

'I'm never going to say that!'

'And kindly let go of my chin,' she seethed. 'Physical intimidation is the cheapest of tricks.'

Immediately he did as she asked. But, rather than letting his hand fall to his side, he drew it lingeringly across her jawline and down the slender line of her neck until it rested on the curve of her shoulder. Something must have flared in her eyes. He said silkily, 'Another cheap trick, I do admit. But it proves you don't feel any more civilised than I.'

Paige would have had difficulty analysing her emotions. What she did know was that she felt fully alive in a way she had not felt for months; it was not altogether a pleasant sensation. With a calmness she was far from feeling, she removed his hand from her shoulder, stepped around him to put more distance between them, and said with an ease she was quite proud of, 'Why don't we go back to the beginning of this conversation—the sandwich? It might be the only issue we'll be able to solve.'

'While it's very kind of you to offer me some of my own food in my own house, I fear I shall have to decline. Where's the boy?'

Her big brown eyes met his. 'Asleep in your bed. What are you planning to have for supper?'

'A domesticated woman?' he hazarded, with a devastating lift of his brow. 'Quite a rarity in these liberated times. I was thinking of barbecuing one pork chop, Miss Montgomery.'

'Make it three, and I'll cook the vegetables and make a salad . . . my Caesar's salad is the rage of San Francisco.'

'Unfortunately the way to this particular man's heart is not through his stomach.'

'So you admit you have a heart?' Paige gave him a captivating smile. 'We make progress, Mr Renshaw.'

For a moment she would have sworn an unwilling smile tugged at her lips. then he said coldly, 'Illusory progress, my dear. This conversation had been very amusing, and I retract my doubts as to your intelligence—but nothing has changed. I do not want you here. I do not want the boy here. Do you understand those two rather elementary facts?'

She flashed back, 'All this isolation isn't good for you—repetition and redundancy were never your trade-marks,' and knew as soon as the words were out that she had made a mistake.

Violent anger underlying each word, he snarled, 'I'm warning you—stay away from the subject of my writing! Or you'll be out of here so fast, you won't know what hit you.'

Genuinely afraid, Paige only wanted to remove herself from his presence. 'If you'll let me get my sandwich, I'll eat outside,' she muttered. As he moved away from the counter, she grabbed the plate and ran.

Once outside, Paige stationed herself near Brent's window so she would hear him when he woke, and gazed at the mountains. She had learned Travis Renshaw's vulnerable point, she thought, waiting for her heartbeat to settle down to normal. But she was quite sure she would never have the nerve to use it.

Supper was an uneasy compromise. Travis barbecued the chops outside, Paige prepared everything else in the kitchen, and they ate at the pine table, making stilted conversation that skirted any issue of real importance. Travis insisted on helping her clear up afterwards. They stood side by side at the sink, Paige washing the dishes, Travis drying them, she silent because she could think of nothing to say, his the silence of hostility. As she passed him the last saucepan, she said desperately, 'Travis, can't we call a truce? We're adults . . . surely we can at least be pleasant to each other?'

'Why should I do anything that might encourage you to stay?' he asked, methodically wiping the saucepan.

'Because we might be good for you.' Paige searched for a knife in the bowl; she had not known she was going to say that.

There was no doubt of his hostility this time. 'You over-estimate you importance,' he said offensively. 'The sooner you both leave, the better I'll like it—got that, Miss Montgomery?'

He hung up the towel and left the room. Paige let the water swirl down the sink, rather glad she did not have to come up with a reply. Maybe, she thought miserably, the passage of time would ease the situation. Maybe . . .

However, the passage of time only served to increase Paige's frustration. She had arrived in Teko Bay very tired and although she managed to sneak a number of catnaps through the day, the tiredness was from months of overwork and not so easily cured. Brent, simply by being a five-year-old, demanded a lot of energy. So Travis's obdurate refusal to give anything of himself other than a minimal politeness grated on her nerves more and more, exacerbated by a very small cabin in which three people could not possibly avoid one another. Travis slept twenty feet away from her. He shaved at the sink. He shared the evening meal with them. She awoke one afternoon from a nap in the hammock near the vegetable garden to find him staring at her inscrutably; and sometimes, when she was playing with Brent outdoors, she sensed him watching them from somewhere in the woods.

A week after she had arrived, she had a rare afternoon to herself. Brent was at the Camerons', playing with the girls; rowdy games, Paige knew, in which he got healthily dirty and talked non-stop, as though he had months of silence to make up for. She was growing very fond of him, which rather frightened her. She herself was in the clearing behind the paddock at Travis's. Among the few books in the cabin were field guides to the flowers and birds of the area, and she was trying to teach herself to recognise some of them; the flowers, she had concluded, were easier because they stayed put.

It was a warm afternoon, with enough of a breeze to keep the mosquitoes down, so she had tied her blue shirt—of which she was growing heartily tired—beneath her breasts, and had rolled her trouser legs above her knees. The sun felt wonderful on her bare skin. Seated in the midst of several clumps of flowers, she opened the field guide. Monkshood, purple as Brent's eyes, was not difficult to identify, nor were the tall, rose-pink spikes of fireweed. Pleased with herself, she picked some of each and stuffed them down the front of her blouse, a few minutes later tucking a sprig of golden cinquefoil behind one ear and weaving a necklace of what she would have called daisies but the book called chrysanthemums. She felt very happy. She had absolutely no responsibilities. No delinquent boys. No forms to be filed in quadruplicate. No screaming mothers. No absentee fathers.

No guilt, she added airily to herself, dropping the chrysanthemums over her head and finding a woolly, magenta-coloured flower that seemed to go by the unprepossessing name of lousewort. She was frowning at the picture in the book when she heard footsteps approach through the trees. Travis stepped into the clearing.

Enter the absentee father, thought Paige. I can't get away from them.

He said sarcastically, 'Are you planning on entering the Rose Bowl Parade?'

She had forgotten about the flowers. Getting to her feet and giving him a brilliant smile, she held up the cluster of magenta blossoms. 'Lousewort?'

He did not even glance at her offering. 'I've been wanting to talk to you,' he said harshly. 'I realised something this morning—you've been here a week. Seven days too long. When are you going to admit you're beaten and leave?'

Paige had been happy; and with a few careless words he had destroyed that happiness. 'Please, Travis, let up for once,' she begged. 'This place is so beautiful, don't spoil it.'

'It will be more beautiful when you've gone.'

Something deep within her snapped. She flung the flower at his chest, her brown eyes pools of rage. 'I cannot leave until you allow Brent to live with you—how many times do I have to tell you that? So the next move's yours, not mine. And in the meantime I wish you'd damn well try behaving like a normal human being——'

'I don't——'

'—or have you forgotten how in this self-imposed exile of yours? I am sick to *death* of being treated like a stick of furniture or an aged auntie who's outstayed her welcome. I'm neither one, I just happen to be someone with a conscience who cares what happens to a small boy, and don't you think that in the last week I've wished I was anyone—or anywhere—else? But I'm not. I'm stuck with myself, Mr Travis Renshaw. So I'm stuck here. And apart from anything else, this is the first vacation I've had in over two years and you're *ruining* it!'

The flowers she had thrust in her shirt were bobbing up and down with her agitated breathing, and the cinquefoil had tipped over her ear. But Paige was too angry to care. Hands on her hips, she glared at him, daring him to laugh at her.

For several seconds Travis said nothing; she had no idea what he was thinking. Then he said slowly, 'You really mean that, don't you? About your conscience. You're not staying here out of stubbornness or pride or sheer cussedness . . . you're staying because you'd be untrue to yourself if you left.'

Paige let out her breath in a long sigh. 'You've got it,' she said.

He was frowning. 'Don't misunderstand me,' he said carefully. 'Nothing's changed as far as the boy is concerned. But I've been guilty of misjuding you—and for that, I'm sorry.'

It was a victory, if only a minor one, in what Paige was beginning to see could be a very protracted war. She tilted her chin. 'So does that mean we can have a reasonable conversation at the dinner table?' she asked.

With a glint in his eyes he said, 'You shall no longer be treated as Great-Aunt Bertha. Come here, Paige.'

It was the first time he had called her by name. She took two steps towards him. His face expressionless, he took the cinquefoil from her ear and tucked it into the neck of her blouse, his fingers brushing the swell of her breast. 'That's better,' he said. Then he bent to pick up the magenta flowers. '*Pedicularis sudectica*,' he added. 'Sudeten lousewort. Rather a dreadful name for such a pretty flower, isn't it?'

Paige suddenly discovered that she liked him very much, and that she badly wanted to touch him. She settled for holding out her hand. 'So it's a truce?' she asked.

His hand clasped hers firmly; his palm was callused. 'Truce,' he said.

She pulled her hand free, filled with the crazy wish that he would take her in his arms and kiss her, terrified that he would read her mind. 'I'd better go and get Brent,' she stammered. 'I—I'm glad we had this talk, Travis.' Then she turned on her heel and ran, shedding flowers as she went.

Paige had assumed this talk with Travis would clear the air; and in a way it did. The tension in the cabin lessened perceptibly. Meals became far more enjoyable, because they began exchanging ideas on any number of topics. In particular Travis began telling her some of the history of the area, about the gold rush in Nelson's Landing at the turn of the century; when paddle-boats had plied the lake and the tents of miners had crowded the shores.

He had a wide-ranging mind and was always interesting.

But he never talked about himself, and he never addressed Brent by name. His refusal to deal with the boy infuriated Paige, yet she had no idea how to bring them together.

The other problem, Paige acknowledged on her ninth evening in the cabin as she stood at the window, watching Travis at his usual task of splitting wood, was uniquely her own. She had never been so physically attracted to a man in her life.

She picked up the bird book, lay down on the couch and began thumbling through the pages. But the brightly coloured pictures failed to hold her interest, and her thoughts marched on. She could sense the exact moment Travis came into the room. She could feel his body warmth when they stood side by side at the sink, doing the dishes. She had craved to touch his bare shoulder the other day when he had come in from the shower.

You're suffering from sexual deprivation, the social worker in her proclaimed coldly. You haven't looked at a man since your brother died, because you haven't had the energy. Travis is a very attractive man who also happens to be sexually deprived; he admitted as much. Do you wonder that there are vibes between you? Perfectly natural. Just don't dress it up as romance. And don't act on it.

Go away, she thought crossly. I'm not going to act on it. Nor am I the slightest bit in love with the man. Ridiculous idea.

She punched the cushion, closed the book and her eyes, and made herself remember the bald eagle she had seen that morning, the air beating against its wings as it hovered near the mouth of the river that connected the inlet with Lake Tahini. Trite to think of it as a symbol of freedom, she thought muzzily. Yet how it belonged to the racing ice-cold waters of the river and the spruce-covered cliffs, a creature of ancient lakes and limitless skies . . .

'Paige, I want to go to bed.'

'Me, too,' she mumbled.

'There isn't room for both of us.'

She fumbled with the cushion, trying to shut out the voice. 'Leave me alone.'

'I won't sleep with the boy.'

The ugly words made her eyes fly open. 'It's dark,' she said stupidly.

'Get up and go to bed.'

Her father had never used that tone of voice to her. Paige sat up, rubbing her eyes so she could focus on Travis. Cause him maximum irritation, Felix had advised when she had first arrived here. She was obviously succeeding; which was no reason she shouldn't try harder. It might even take her mind off sex. 'The boy has a name,' she said.

'Don't start that now!'

'Your name. Renshaw. Would it be so awful if you had to share a bed with him?'

'I'd much rather share it with you,' Travis answered, so that for a horrible moment Paige wondered if she had said the word 'sex' out loud. Kneeling beside the couch, he ran a finger from her cheekbone to her chin then leaned forward and kissed her on the mouth, his lips lingering, searching for a response.

The shock ran through her whole body. Mesmerised, her eyes wide open, she watched him move back and saw the confidence, the urge to dominate, in the strongly hewn features. 'You mustn't *do* that!' she sputtered.

'It's been a long time since a man's kissed you, hasn't it, Paige? Why? Do those ironbound principles of yours extend to sex as well?'

In delayed reaction, the adrenalin was now racing through her veins. But Paige had no intention of talking about sex. She adjusted the cushion behind her back and said, 'You dislike my principles because they've incon- venienced you—you would much have preferred me to have taken Brent away and left you undisturbed in your fake little paradise.'

She had touched him on the raw. 'There's nothing fake about the life I lead!'

'No? Then why are there so few books in the house?'

'I don't have the time to read.'

She pressed to the attack, remembering his vulnerable point. 'You're a writer, and writers live by books. I haven't even found the book you wrote five years ago. You're not just running away from Stephanie and Brent up here, Travis, you're running away from yourself.'

He gripped her wrist, his face only inches from hers. 'I wrote one book. That's all. One book doesn't make a writer.'

'Have you ever tried to write another one?'

'No!'

In the faint silver radiance that was coming in the window from the moon, Paige could see the torment in his eyes. This was not a conversation she had planned or even anticipated, and certainly it had nothing to do with sex; yet she was so sure the words needed to be said that she hardened her heart against his pain and said fiercely, 'I've read your book and I've read what the critics said about it—you don't need me to tell you that you're immensely talented and that you're wasting those talents chopping wood and growing beans.'

His nails dug into her wrist. 'Have you quite finished?'

'Travis,' she said gently, 'someone had to say it.'

'Nothing in our acquaintance gives *you* the right! What I do—or don't do—in my personal life is my business, and mine alone. Do you understand that?'

Paige refused to back down. 'As far as your writing is concerned, I regret it; as far as Brent is concerned, I abhor it.'

She had not raised her voice, and her brown eyes met his bravely. Releasing her wrist, he sat back on his heels and took a deep breath. 'You're a fighter, aren't you? And you're honest, I'll give you that. Honesty isn't always an attribute of the legal profession.'

'I'm not a lawyer,' she said, surprised. 'A friend of mine who's a lawyer asked me to bring Brent up here. I'm a social worker.'

'Ah . . . solving the world's problems from behind a desk,' he said caustically. 'But I'm not on your caseload, Paige—you might do well to remember that.'

She sat up straight, her cheeks flushed. 'In every profession there are those who hide behind their desks. I don't happen to be one of them.'

'So what do you do? Rush out into the streets, looking for errant writers to convert?'

'No! I work with adolescent boys, a lot of them homeless because their parents don't want them, nearly all of them on drugs, most of them petty criminals . . . I try and keep them out of the clutches of the pimps and the prostitutes and the dealers, and I fail much more often than I succeed. *That's* what I do!'

Although she had been shaking with indignation, her shoulders suddenly sagged. She added flatly, 'Very clever, Mr Renshaw. You made me so angry that I told you far more than I'd intended to.'

He did not bother denying it. 'Is your job the reason you arrived here exhausted?'

My job and my brother. 'Yes.'

'I've been watching you—every time you sit down, you fall asleep.'

She said weakly, 'I didn't think you were interested enough to watch me.'

'I'm becoming more interested by the minute.'

'I have a feeling that to be ignored by you might be safer.'

'Oh, safety,' he said impatiently. 'You and I both seem to have opted for safety as far as the opposite sex is concerned, haven't we? You've buried yourself in your job and I've buried myself in the wilderness. But is safety what we really want?'

Abruptly he stood up, pulled her to her feet and took her round the pine table to the window. The moonlight shone on the perplexity in her face and on the lustrous brown eyes; her skin seemed to glow with a radiance of its own. He bent his head and kissed her again.

This time Paige was not taken by surprise, and his kiss filled her with a wild, sweet longing. He had made no attempt to embrace her; he had not needed to, she thought shakily.

'Well?' he said

She searched his face for any sign of emotion and found none. 'What are you asking, Travis?'

'I want to make love to you, Paige.'

With an immense effort, she neither blushed nor looked away. 'We can't,' she said with a ghost of a smile. 'Brent is in the bed.'

'He could stay at Felix's tomorrow. Or we could go outdoors.'

'We can't,' she repeated, more wildly. 'All we've done is fight ever since we met.'

'Safety, Paige?' he mocked. 'You're a risk-taker. Or you wouldn't be doing the job you are.'

'You have no idea why I do my job,' she said soberly. 'Any more than I understand why you're not doing yours. We don't know each other at all. We can't just hop into bed!'

'I would have thought that was as good a place as any to get to know someone,' he said harshly.

'Or could it be just another hiding place? A place to avoid the real issues—like Brent.'

'You're obsessed with that boy! We're talking about you and me—not him.'

'He came with me, and he has to stay with you . . . we can't get away from him,' she answered, and felt confusion twist her heart. For he was right. She *was* a risk-taker. She wanted to go to bed with him, to learn about him in the most elemental way possible between a man and a woman. She, who had had not a handful of dates in the past two years, and all of them chaste . . . what was happening to her?

'You're the one who's hiding, Paige. Brent's just another homeless boy, isn't he? An extension of your job. An excuse to avoid intimacy.'

She flinched, and said in a low voice, 'Is it intimacy you're offering me, Travis? Or is it sex?'

He raked his fingers through his hair. With complete un-expectedness he said, 'I like you, Paige Montgomery—you call it as you see it, don't you?' He hesitated. 'Will you answer one question for me?'

His unforeseen compliment had warmed her; she nodded. He said. 'Do you want to go to bed with me?'

She raised her head, her cheekbones tinged with colour, and gave the only possible reply. 'Yes.'

'Thank you,' he said simply.

She wanted to say many things; that they had made tremendous strides that night in the elusive quality called intimacy; that he was finally seeing her as a real person and not merely as the purveyor of Brent; that she, against all the odds, liked him. She said none of them. Instead she brought her palm up to his cheek and rested it there briefly. He too was real. A man of flesh and blood. A complicated, subtle man. A man on the run . . .

He brought her palm to his lips. 'It's late,' he said. 'You'd better go to bed.'

Without him. But would it always be that way? Her lashes hiding her eyes, she murmured, 'Goodnight, Travis.'

'Goodnight.'

As she crossed the floor and climbed the stairs to the

bedroom, Paige knew that he was watching her. She undressed in the dark, aware of every small noise he made on the other side of the door; and her body ached to be held by him.

The next morning, for the first time since they had arrived at Teko Bay, Paige woke up before Brent. A light rain was pattering on the roof. She never drew the curtains here, and through the glass she could see the silvery raindrops clinging to the tips of the pine boughs, like tear-shaped ear-rings.

In his sleep Brent had sought the warmth of her body, so that he was lying in the crook of her arm. She rested her cheek on his tumbled brown curls and felt a surge of protective love for him. She wanted him to be happy; and happiness for Brent meant Teko Bay.

Her arm must have tightened unconsciously. He wriggled in protest and woke up. 'Hi, Paige,' he mumbled. 'C'n I get up yet?'

A week ago he would have pulled away from her and given her one of his baleful looks. She nuzzled her face into his neck. 'I guess so.'

He was already scrambling across her. 'I gotta go and see the kittens.'

The tabby cat that lived in the barn had obliged by having four kittens the day after she and Brent had arrived. 'Put on your jacket and boots,' Paige said. Fiona, who was bigger than Brent, was luckily a source of secondhand clothes.

She could hear him grunting as he struggled with the zipper on his jeans, and leaned over to help him with the snap and with the toggles on his rain-jacket. 'Have fun,' she said.

He bounded down the steps, and a moment later she heard the cabin door bang shut. Travis would have been up long ago; she sometimes thought he got up early to avoid them.

Pulling the duvet up to her chin, Paige allowed herself

to recall every detail of her strange encounter with Travis in the moonlight. Although she had no idea where they would go from there, she did not doubt they would go somewhere. You couldn't go backwards from intimacy, she thought, and felt an upwelling of anticipation. Everything would work out. It had to.

She got out of bed and dressed in her new jeans and a smocked cotton top that Nell had loaned her, a very pretty top made of natural cotton embroidered in shades of green and rust that flattered Paige's colouring. After washing in cold water at the sink, a routine she was actually getting used to, she put cream on her face, dabbed on some perfume, and made the bed. Then she went into the living-room, where she stood by the window and gazed out at the mountains. That, too, had become part of her routine. This morning the peaks were shrouded in mist, while the grass in the paddock was startlingly green, as if the kiss of the rain had brought it new life. Travis was walking from the paddock to the barn.

Her pulse jumped. He was wearing jeans, workboots and an old checked shirt, and was carrying a bucket: not a figure of romance. But her blood was racing in her veins and she felt as breathless as if she had been running. This man, walking in his wilderness domain with such loose-limbed grace, wanted her. Desired her. Liked her. She found she was smiling.

Brent burst out of the barn door, running as fast as his legs would carry him, just as Travis came round the corner of the barn. Brent cannoned into him.

The little boy fell flat on the ground. Travis instinctively reached out a hand to help him up. But then the gesture froze in mid-air.

Paige drew a sharp breath. Help him to get up . . . you've got to help him, she urged silently.

Travis straightened, his hands tight at his sides. Brent picked himself up, circling around the man as warily as if Travis were a grizzly bear. Then he broke into a run, racing for the cabin as though his life depended on it.

Travis stood still, watching him. Then he turned his back and with shocking violence pounded his fist once, twice, against the corner of the barn.

Sick to her soul, Paige buried her face in her hands. This was the man she wanted to make love to, this man who could not bring himself to touch his son. How could he be so cruel, so uncaring?

Brent's boots thumped into the porch. She heard him kick them off; he had not inherited his father's tidiness. He tumbled over the step into the room and cried, 'The cat's moved the kittens to another place!'

She conjured up a degree of enthusiasm. 'That's exciting—where did she put them?'

'In the loft. Under the hay.'

'Did you hurt yourself when you fell?'

'Nope.' He pulled a hideous face. 'He doesn't like me, does he?'

And what was she to say to that? 'I thought he was starting to. But now I don't know any more.' All the progress she thought they had made was an illusion, she decided wearily. Travis was no nearer accepting Brent as his son than he had been ten days ago.

'What's for breakfast?' said Brent, as he plunked himself down at the table.

It was obvious that she was more upset by the incident than Brent was. 'Oatmeal, as soon as I make it,' she answered, and headed for the kitchen.

The two of them were sitting at the table, eating, when Travis came in the door. Brent lifted his head, milk dribbling down his chin. His jaw jutting, he scowled at the man. Travis stared right back, his jaw set at exactly the same angle.

Had the issue been less important, Paige might have

laughed. Or at least kept quiet. 'Travis,' she cried with complete conviction, 'can't you see how alike the two of you are? Can't you see that you belong to each other?'

He transferred his unyielding, steel-blue gaze to her. 'No,' he snapped, 'I can't. Why don't you mind your own business?'

She could not start a fight with Brent present. To relieve her feelings, she tugged at her hair, rolled her eyes ceiling-ward, heard Brent giggle and said evenly, 'There's tea on the stove. Help yourself.' Then she went back to her oat-meal. Maybe anticipation should always be distrusted, she thought glumly. As should sexual attraction.

Travis poured his tea and went outside, and Paige knew as clearly as if he had announced it that she would not see him again until supper time. She washed the dishes, did a little perfunctory dusting, then took Brent to the Camerons'. Nell was busy at her loom, and Felix was in his workroom with the door closed; feeling as if she could earn her keep for once, Paige fingerpainted with the children all morning, and after lunch, since the rain had thinned to a fine mist, she took them to play in the brook.

When she and Brent went home, he was as happy as he was muddy. She fried caribou steak for supper, made artificial conversation with Travis as they ate, and was heartily glad when he went outdoors again. She would read when Brent was in bed, she thought. But she would not fall asleep on the couch.

However, she could not settle to a book. The cabin was so deadly quiet that in a sudden pang of homesickness Paige longed for the clamour and confusion of her apartment building in the city, and the demands of her job. In San Francisco she was useful. She could accomplish something. There was not a hope of that here. Restlessly she got up from her chair and went outside. It had stopped raining. She would walk down to the river and see if the eagles were there.

Cinquefoil, monkshood and fireweed still edged the path. Warblers burbled in the alders. She took a detour, following an elusive flash of yellow feathers, discovering instead an old stone wall running from the woods down to the river. The noise of the water grew louder and louder, and the ground became spongy with moisture. She stepped into the clearing at the riverbank.

Travis was standing on the little dock, holding a fishing-rod. The rod was bent, the line singing with tension; his feet were braced. The two eagles were perched high on the opposite bank.

Paige could have retreated; he had not seen her. Instead she yelled, 'You've got an audience of three now,' and saw him start. 'What have you caught?'

He threw her a sudden boyish grin and shouted, 'Nothing yet!'

Encouraged by this tacit dropping of hostilities, Paige went closer. Travis was slowly reeling the fish in, the muscles in his forearms bulging with the strain. Over the splash and roar of the water he grunted, 'Tomorrow's supper—Arctic grayling. If I can land him.'

The small spurt of spray where the line entered the water was closer now. 'Can I do anything to help?'

'Take the net—when I bring him up to the dock, try and scoop him up in it.'

The fish's tail broke the surface only a couple of feet from the wharf. The next few seconds were highly exciting. Somehow Paige got the net around the writhing body without falling in the river, and then she and Travis hauled the fish up on the wooden planks, during which process she got very wet. Travis cracked the fish hard on the head and it lay still.

It was large and scaly and very dead; its bulbous eyes seemed to stare at her in reproach. She said, 'Maybe I'll be out for supper tomorrow night.'

'I could insist that you clean it and cook it.'

She shuddered. 'No, thanks.'

He was laughing at her, his teeth white against his tan. 'You'd rather face a drug dealer.'

'Any good honest criminal would be preferable to that,' she said primly.

'So when I serve it poached in white wine with a hollandaise sauce, you'll have a peanut butter sandwich?'

She wrinkled her nose. 'Keep talking.'

'How did you get so wet, Paige?'

Paige looked down at herself. The front of her cotton smock was soaked, clinging to her breasts. She blushed a fiery red. 'Damned fish,' she muttered.

'Paige . . .'

His arms were around her, drawing her close to his chest; the river seethed in her ears, and before she closed her eyes she saw one of the eagles soar across the water. She slid her palms up Travis's damp shirt and gave herself up to his kiss, her body as pliant as the willow trees along the river's edge, whose branches hung over the tumultuous, rushing waves.

It was a deep kiss, that spoke uncompromisingly of Travis's loneliness and separation. With every nerve in her body Paige wanted to comfort him, to end the isolation she had sensed in him from the start. Straining on tiptoes, she caressed his scalp, the strong cords of his neck, the breadth of his shoulders under the checked shirt, responding to him with all the generosity of which she was capable.

When his hand found the softness of her breast under her smock, a quiver ran through her frame. He eased away from her, his eyes trained on the changing expressions in her face as he stroked the fullness of her flesh. She felt no shame; only wonderment and a desire so acute as to be unbearable.

When he spoke, the same passionate need roughened his voice. 'Paige, I've got to make love to you—I've got to. You don't know how much I want you.'

She did know, for it was written on his face and blazed in his eyes. 'I want you too,' she said, and knew words had never been more useless to express how she was feeling.

Like a man who had temporarily lost his bearings, he looked around him. 'We can't stay here.'

'We'd drown,' she said unsteadily.

He gave her a sudden hug. 'I love the way you make me laugh.'

She would have sworn there was tenderness in his voice, and felt a fragile, piercing happiness well up within her. The happiness, she thought confusedly, seemed more important than the lovemaking. Or did the one depend on the other?

Travis grabbed her hand. 'Come on.'

The fish lay forgotten on the dock as he led her along the path, past the wild flowers, so vivid and so short-lived. The old packhorse, whose name was Bentley, whickered a greeting to them as they neared the paddock. The cabin came into view, where Brent was sleeping. But Travis was taking her towards the barn.

Paige felt her footsteps slow, and was aware of being cold under her wet blouse. As they came to the corner of the barn where Travis had pounded his fist against the logs, she knew with complete illogic that she did not want to make love anywhere near there. She blurted, 'Travis, when Brent bumped into you this morning, why didn't you pick him up?'

He dropped her hand. 'So you were watching . . .' She nodded, watching the strain gather in his face. 'I can't bring myself to touch him,' he said violently.

'That was self-evident,' she replied with a wry twist of her mouth. 'But why not?'

'Every time I look at him I see Stephanie . . . her eyes, her hair, even her air of defiance.'

'The air of defiance is yours.'

'You keep saying that—but in the note she left, she swore

the child was not mine.'

'A note? You mean she didn't tell you in person?'

'No,' he said shortly. 'I came home one day to find her gone, and a nice explanatory letter lying on the bed. Written in green ink. Smelling of her perfume.'

Despite Barbara's defence, Paige had never liked the sound of Stephanie, and now she liked her even less. 'You've never forgiven her, have you?' she said straight-forwardly.

'Look, I haven't seen her for five years, and she's dead now—that part of my life is a closed chapter.'

'Brent's reopened it.'

'Brent is not my son!'

Her eyes glittered. 'There—you said his name. The sky didn't fall, did it?'

Travis said tightly, 'It's a wonder to me that none of your clients in San Francisco has never bopped you on the head and dumped you in the harbour, Miss Paige Montgomery.'

Paige took a step backwards; he rather looked as if he would like to follow that course of action himself. 'I can run fast,' she said.

'Then why don't you run right out of sight?' he suggested unpleasantly. 'Because I no longer have the slightest desire to make love to you.'

She could see the tangled dark hair in the open neckline of his shirt and the throbbing pulse at the base of his throat, and, knew that against all odds she still wanted to make love to him. So much for her principles. Here was a man whose behaviour she deplored, and she would jump into bed with him at the first kiss. If there were a bed, she thought crazily. Classic case of a roll in the hay.

None of which she cared to say. 'You just want a woman who agrees with every word you say and thinks everything you do is marvellous . . . I'm not like that.'

'Another self-evident truth.'

Paige very much wanted to burst into tears; but she had a sneaking suspicion that was what Stephanie would have done. 'Did it help to pound your fist on the side of the barn?' she asked.

Unwillingly, Travis smiled. 'Just don't break any bones—we're long way from a doctor.' As she glared at him, he added, 'And don't be tempted to substitute me for the barn.'

'You've got about as much feeling,' Paige retorted childishly.

'Don't push me on that one, either.'

All too clearly she remembered the strength of his embrace, the ardour of his kiss, and shivered. 'I'm going to check on Brent,' she said stiffly.

'Good. I'm glad to see you take your responsibilities so seriously.'

She blushed, for both of them knew that down on the dock Brent had not been her main concern. 'Go get the fish, Travis,' she said crossly. 'I want to eat tomorrow night.'

'Yes . . . it might be your only chance for grayling. Your vacation's running out, isn't it?'

There was mockery in the blue eyes, and an element of threat as well. Paige could think of nothing to say. He was right. The days were passing all too quickly; and nothing was resolved. With a small gesture of frustration that was more telling than words, she turned away from him and walked towards the cabin.

CHAPTER FOUR

'IS TRAVIS any nearer to accepting Brent as his son?' Nell asked thoughtfully, watching the three children play in the sandpit. 'You've been here over a week now.'

'No. Travis would like me and Brent to disappear as thoroughly as Stephanie did,' Paige said bitterly.

'Is there nothing you can do?'

'I've tried screaming at him and I've tried the sweet voice of reason—he's oblivious to both.'

Nell's serenity was painly ruffled. 'Brent's a dear little boy. I don't understand Travis.'

'I think he's still in love with Stephanie—so he can't get beyond her,' Paige said with painful truth; it was a conclusion she had reached after much soul-searching. Travis wanted her sexually, there was a question about that, but he had never mentioned any of the gentler emotions. Those he still reserved for his dead wife.

'I wish we could help.'

'Nell dear, you do,' Paige said warmly. 'You've given Brent a wonderful experience of family life that I swear he's never had before. While I know I've made four new friends.'

Nell gave her an unaffected hug. 'I'll hate to see you leave. Couldn't you take more holidays?'

Restlessly Paige got up from her chair. 'What would that accomplish? Oh, Nell, I don't know what to do . . . I'm in limbo. No good to anyone. I'm getting far too fond of Brent, and Travis doesn't want anything to do with either of us.'

'When I feel that way, I go for a walk in the woods,' Nell declared. 'I'll give the children their lunch—off you go.'

Because she had felt responsible for Brent, Paige had done very little exploring. 'Are you sure . . .?'

Nell made shooing motions. 'Of course I am. You could head north along the shore of the inlet, away from Travis's. It's sandy for at least a mile, and there are some pretty coves.'

Away from Travis . . . that was what she needed, thought Paige, as she set off a few minutes later, arrayed in a pair of Nell's shorts and carrying her lunch in a paper bag. She followed the trail until it ended at Felix's dock, the breeze lifting her hair and the sun blazing from a cloudless sky. Away from Travis . . . she set off down the shore.

The glitter of mica in the white sand made her wonder if miners waiting for the train had ever searched for gold along the shore. When she came to a creek, she clambered up its rocky bed for quite a way, not really sure what she was looking for, although an image of a large, wrinkled gold nugget sitting tidily in the middle of the stream had a tendency of persist in her mind. The trees cast a pattern of mingled light and shadow on the bubbling waters, and it was very peaceful under the canopy of beech and pine. With a wonderful sense of release, she realised that no one knew exactly where she was. Not Brent, with his big violet eyes that constantly reminded her of his parentage. And not Travis. She sat down on a smooth, mossy boulder to think about Travis.

For a woman of twenty-three, living in one of the most permissive cities in the country, Paige was relatively in-experienced. She had been briefly engaged during her junior year in university to a young man named Harold, whose *nouveaux riches* parents had disapproved of her more modest background. By applying the most basic financial leverage to their son, they had persuaded him to feel the same way. He had had golden hair, a California tan and oodles of charm; he had also had a beautiful body. Before the concerted descent of his parents, they had spent a weekend in a resort hotel in San Diego. Although Paige could remember the palm trees on the beach and the ten different kinds of tropical fruit that had been served for breakfast, she had great difficulty remembering their lovemaking.

It had failed to touch the centre of her being, she mused. Her soul, for want of a better word. She had been dazzled and charmed and flattered by Harold's attentions, but she had never really loved him. She had discovered that truth when his parents had broken up the match. Her pride had been hurt, and she had been furious that he had given in so easily, but she had never felt like jumping off the Golden Gate Bridge, and had even been aware of a truant sense of relief.

She pulled apart a clump of moss with her fingernails. Without knowing why, she was sure Travis would touch her soul. Perhaps that was why she was so attracted to him, and yet simultaneously so afraid of him.

Another four days and she would be leaving. So why was she worrying?

Paige stood up, her sneaker slipping on a rock and plunging her foot into the frigid water. This was no place to break an ankle, she thought, and determinedly put Travis out of her mind.

In the next hour she saw several deer tracks, two squirrels, four unknown birds and no gold nuggets. Enjoying herself thoroughly, she found a cove sheltered from the breeze and sat down on the grass to eat her sandwich. Then she knelt by the edge of the inlet to drink from it. The water was crystal-clear. She could see her own reflection, her wide brown eyes seeming to ask a question of her . . .

'You look like Narcissus kneeling by the pool.'

Paige stayed crouched, for she knew whose voice it was, and with a strange sense of inevitability was scarcely even startled. She heard the soft crunch of footsteps in the yielding sand. Then another reflection joined hers in the clear water.

Travis. Who else could it be?

Paige smiled, and her image smiled with her. 'How did you know where I was?' she murmured.

'I didn't. I was checking my woodlot on the north side of the peninsula and decided to come here for a drink. It's a favourite place of mine.'

She was glad he had not followed her, that fate rather than intention had brought them together. 'I'll give you a drink,' she said.

He knelt beside her. She cupped her hands in the lake then lifted them up, the water trickling through her fingers. Bending his head, he drank. The sunlight glistened in his hair. 'It's cold, isn't it?' she said.

'Best water in the world.'

His eyes met hers and she knew the words were irrelevant, having nothing to do with what was between them. Travis put a hand under her elbow and lifted her to her feet; his arm around her, he led her to the grassy embankment. Then he kissed her.

At the first touch of his tongue she parted her lips, wanting to withhold nothing. Her searching fingers found the hardness of bone under his thick hair, and the taut muscles of his nape, and all the while he was kissing her, until any remnants of fear were lost in an aching hunger.

This time when he drew back he did not seek her breast beneath her shirt, but undid the buttons one by one, then pulled the garment open. The shadow of his body fell across her pale skin and the small, perfect breasts; colour rose in her cheeks at the intentness of his gaze. She eased the shirt from her shoulders and let it drop to the ground.

As if each movement were part of a primitive choreography, they undressed in utter silence. Paige knew they were alone in their wilderness paradise, her nakedness as natural as the caress of the sun and the breeze on her back. Travis guided her down beside him on the grass, spreading his shirt for her to lie on, and still without saying a word let his hands travel the length of her body, as though to memorise its every curve.

She lay entranced, for his touch seemed to confirm her existence in some way she had always needed without knowing why. His rhythmic stroking made her real, more truly herself than she had ever been before . . . could it be possible she could confer upon him the same gift?

Wanting to do so more than anything else in the world, she slid her palms down the hair-roughened chest, with exquisite sensitivity tracing the hard breastbone and the taut, concave belly, the ridge of his hip and the curve of buttock. She heard his sharp, indrawn breath; but still he did not speak. Putting his arms around her, he brought her close, so that they were joined from shoulder to knee.

She felt his arousal with fierce pride, and opened her thighs to gather him in. He smiled at her, his blue eyes like fragments of the lake, eyes in which she could drown. Taking his time, he let his mouth drift down her throat to her nipple. In a surge of emotion she could not have defined, she held the tousled head to her breast and knew she was in heaven.

But then he entered her and heaven was not enough. Her body convulsed. Head thrown back, she gave an inarticulate cry that was swallowed by the watching forest. Slowly he began to move within her. But she matched him thrust for thrust, joying in him, until the exultation in his face and the agony of his desire were her own. A sunburst of colour that throbbed behind her lids became the throb of his release and her own inexorable fulfilment; and the spell that had fallen on them on the shore of the inlet gave of its magic.

Paige lay very still, lost to herself in the circle of Travis's arms. He had given her that which she had never received before. She never wanted to let him go. She closed her eyes, enfolded in his warmth, safe from all harm, and drifted off to sleep.

She had a crick in her neck and she was cold.

Slowly Paige sat up. The breeze had freshened, and her flesh was covered in goose-bumps, even though someone had spread her shirt over her.

Travis.

In a flash of memory she remembered everything that had happened. Leaning on her palms, she looked around. The clearing was empty save for herself. The trees waved gently in the wind. The surface of the inlet was ruffled now; she would no longer be able to see her reflection.

Travis was gone.

Paige was enveloped in a cold that had nothing to do with the wind. He couldn't be gone. He couldn't have left her alone after making love to her. The last thing she remembered was falling asleep in his arms, feeling utterly secure, as though she had found the haven she had unconsciously been seeking all her life. It had never occurred to her that he would not be there when she woke up.

Moving awkwardly, because her limbs felt stiff, she shrugged into her shirt and managed to button it. Then she stood up and pulled on her shorts, fumbling with the snap.

A branch cracked in the woods. She whirled, every muscle tense. But there was only the sighing of the wind through the pine boughs and the chatter of the waves on the sand, and she forced herself to relax. After lacing her sneakers and shoving the paper bag that had held her lunch into her pocket, she was ready to leave.

She gave one last look around the clearing. In a pang of sheer terror she suddenly wondered if she had dreamed the whole episode: she had sat down to eat her lunch and she had fallen asleep, and then she had dreamed that a black-haired man had seen her reflection in the water and had taken possession of her, body and soul.

She crossed her arms over her breast, trembling. It couldn't have happened that way. Travis's possession of her, so complete and so beautiful, could not simply be a product of her subconscious, wish-fulfilment in its crudest form. On impulse, Paige ran down to the shore, where with deep relief she saw the imprint of a man's boots in the sand. Travis had been here. She had not dreamed their lovemaking; a real man of flesh and blood had held her in his arms.

He had held her, yes, she thought, staring across the inlet at the indifferent mountains. But he had not spoken to her while they made love. And he had left her alone afterwards.

Paige shivered, still hugging her arms to her chest. The forest seemed to be crowding to the water's edge, as though it wanted to push her in. The inlet mocked her with its brilliant blue sheen, for beneath that sheen lay ice-cold depths, dark as the grave. She was but a speck in the vastness of the wilderness. If she disappeared, who would care? Travis, she cried inwardly, why did you leave?

Abruptly she had the sensation that someone was watching her from deep in the woods, and the hair rose on the back of her neck. She turned, staring into the green-shadowed forest with its ever-shifting patterns of light and dark. No one was there.

Almost running, Paige set off along the shore towards the Camerons. She needed people—the voices of children and Nell's serene smile. People who cared that she existed.

She passed the creek and the dock and scurried up the path to the house. Nell was taking a cranberry cake out of the oven of the wood stove, and the kitchen was very warm. 'How was your walk?' Nell asked, testing the centre of the cake with her finger.

'I looked for gold but I didn't find any, and then I fell asleep,' Paige replied quickly. 'That smells good.'

'We'll have some with a cup of tea. You're probably thirsty.'

'Have you seen Travis?' The question had an underlying tension Paige could not have prevented.

'No, not today. Isn't he supposed to be at home, cooking the fish for you?'

Paige did not want to be reminded of the fish. She busied herself getting the cups and steered Nell on to the subject of making dyes from lichens and weeds for the wool that she wove. Travis was forgotten, at least by Nell.

But Paige could not forget him. As she walked hand in hand with Brent along the track towards the cabin, she was filled with dread. How could she face him? What was she going to say to him? Everything had changed between them . . . surely he would understand that?

Brent tugged at her hand. 'Hurry up, Paige! I want to see the kittens. Beth wants me to give her one, do you think I can?'

'I don't see why not,' said Paige. 'There's the oak tree, we're almost home.'

Then her heart skipped a beat, for Travis was waiting for them in the shade of the oak tree, leaning against the trunk as if he had not a care in the world. Brent saw him in the same instant. 'Going to the barn,' he said breathlessly, and ran straight down the slope as fast as his legs would carry him.

Paige's throat closed with panic as Travis lessened the gap between them with his long, easy strides; he had been chewing on a blade of grass and tossed it casually aside just before he got to her.

The gesture for some reason infuriated her, so that she failed to notice how watchful his eyes were or how taut his jawline. She said clearly, 'When I fell asleep I hadn't expected you to abandon me—fortunately I didn't get attacked by a grizzly.'

'I haven't seen a grizzly around here in three years. Anyway, I was watching you from the woods.'

So it had not been her imagination when she had sensed unseen eyes in the forest. Paige's nostrils flared. He must have watched her every move. In excruciating detail she remembered how bewildered and distressed she had been when she had first discovered she was alone, and how awkwardly she had dragged on her clothes. She had made a fool of herself. And the whole time he had been spying on her.

All the mingled emotions that had been seething in her breast exploded into fury. 'I hope you're proud of yourself! Once you'd got what you wanted it didn't take you long to leave, did it?'

'Don't, Paige——'

'Don't what? Don't confront you with the truth? You couldn't even stay with me until I woke up!'

'It wasn't like that.'

In a deadly quiet voice, her fists clenched at her sides, she said, 'What was it like, Travis?'

He half raised his hands, as though aware of the inadequacy of his words. 'It was beautiful,' he said in a low voice.

She quivered as if he had struck her. 'So beautiful that you couldn't wait to be gone? That you had to spy on me from the woods like a peeping Tom?'

'I wasn't spying! I just wanted to make sure you were safe. Paige, you're twisting the whole thing—when I said it was beautiful, I meant it. *You* were beautiful—more generous than I could ever have expected.' He hesitated, and there was nothing casual in his stance now. 'But it can't happen again.'

Pain ripped through her. She said cuttingly, 'You're assuming that I'd want to.'

'Yes . . . I think it was as beautiful for you as it was for me. You couldn't have faked what happened to you by the shore, Paige.'

To her horror, her voice shook. 'If it was so wonderful, why can't it happen again?'

'You'll be leaving here in a few days, you and the boy. I don't want a casual affair, on one week, off the next. I had a stint of that right after Stephanie left, and it's soul-destroying. I won't do it to myself, and I pay you the compliment of not wanting it for you, either. I don't think you're like that, any more than I am.'

She wasn't, of course. 'Then it should never have happened at all!' she cried, and the pain was raw in her voice.

He did not contradict her. 'For my part in that, I'm sorry.'

Her body was shaking like the leaves of the trembling aspen that grew down by the water. Making love with Travis had been the most real thing she had done in her entire life, for paradoxically her union with him had made her at one with herself. Yet he was snatching that gift from her before she had even had the chance to appreciate it. 'I'm sorry, too—we should never have done it,' she muttered. Her throat tight with tears, she went on desperately, "Travis, I can't stay here now, it's impossible, surely you understand that?'

His mouth thinned. 'What will you do?'

'I'll ask Felix to take me over the lake. The car's still there—I can drive to Whitehorse.' With all her heart, she suddenly longed to be back in her apartment, where everything was familiar and the rules known.

'You and the boy,' Travis said relentlessly.

The four small words shattered Paige's precarious self-control. 'Your son!' she flared. 'Brent is your son, Travis, and you can't send him away—you can't!' He's been happier here than he's ever been before,

I'd swear to it. He belongs here, this is his home, don't you *dare* speak of sending him away. I'll fight you tooth and nail, and anyway, where the *hell* would I take him, just answer me——'

'Shut up!' Travis grabbed her shoulder and gave her a rough shake. 'I won't——'

'You let go of her!' Brent shrilled. 'I hate you!'

Aghast, Paige looked down. The boy was beating his chubby fists against Travis's thigh, tears streaming down his cheeks. 'Brent,' she gasped. 'Brent, don't do that, it's not——'

Travis dropped her shoulder as if the contact were scalding him. 'I didn't mean——'

'I want to stay here with *her*,' the boy interrupted, his little face a rictus of fury. 'Not with you. I wish you'd go away and never come back, 'cause I hate you!'

Dodging Paige's outstretched hand, Brent whirled and careened down the slope towards the barn. As he disappeared around the corner of the cabin, Paige said hopelessly, 'What have we done?'

'Go after him!'

She found that she was crying. Wiping her cheeks, she said in a dead voice, 'And what will I tell him when I find him, Travis?'

'You'd better tell him he can stay.'

She focused through a haze of tears. New lines had carved themselves around the man's mouth; his features were drained of emotion. 'But you don't want him,' she said.

'What the hell else can I do?' he demanded.

Once or twice in the past few days, Paige had allowed herself to imagine Travis's acceptance of Brent as his son, to picture the scene in her mind; it had been very touching. Nothing like the reality. 'Travis, this is all wrong——'

He was staring in the direction Brent had gone, his profile as hard as granite. 'Go after him, Paige.'

'He'll be all right. He's probably crying his eyes out in the hay with the kittens.' She put her hand on Travis's forearm. The skin was warm, and for an instant she was seared by memories so acute that she almost cried out with the pain. Fighting down both memory and pain, for Brent's cause was more important than her feelings, she began, 'Travis, can't you——'

He jerked away from her as though she had stabbed him. 'I said I'll take him, Paige. I don't know why you're complaining—after all, you've won.'

'No one's won. Because you don't really want him.'

He gave a humourless laugh. 'He doesn't want me, either.'

She bit her lip. It was true: Brent hated Travis. To say, You asked for it, would be no help. To say, You're hurt, would be even less appreciated. But Travis *was* hurt, she was sure; and she chose to see this as a note of hope. She said quietly, 'I'll go and find him and tell him he can stay.' But for a moment she remained poised. 'You won't change your mind, though, Travis? It's a serious commitment—you're sure about it?'

'Tell him he can stay,' Travis repeated evenly.

Slowly Paige turned away and began walking down the slope. She *had* won. But her victory felt like ashes in her mouth, and she could find no joy in her heart. 'Brent!' she called as she came round the corner of the cabin. 'Brent, where are you?' She was hardly surprised when he did not answer; she wouldn't have under the same circumstances. Pushing the barn door open, she entered the lofty, sweetly scented darkness.

Something rustled in the hay above her head. 'Brent,' she said softly, 'it's OK, you can come down, it's all settled. You can stay here, Travis says so.'

Silence. 'Do you want me to come up?' she offered, and without waiting for a reply crossed the uneven floorboards to the rickety old ladder. But when she reached the hayloft, searching the gloom for Brent's small figure, all she saw was the mother cat and the squirming heap of kittens half buried in the hay. 'Brent!' she called more sharply. 'Please don't hide, I'm not not in the mood for games.'

Her eyes adjusted to the dim light, she waded through the loosely tossed hay, checking all the corners of the loft, trying to ignore the nibblings of fear. 'Brent, come on out—you can stay here in Teko Bay and you'll be able to play with Beth and Fiona every day. Brent, where *are* you?'

One of the kittens squealed; then the barn was quiet again. Paige could hear the pounding of her own heart as she stood tensely, every sense alert. Brent was not in the barn. No one was in the barn except for herself.

She scrambled down the ladder and ran outside. 'Brent!' she cried. 'Come here, I want you.'

Bentley nickered from the paddock. Chimo and Minto galloped round the cabin, tails waving, jaws agape. Travis was on their heels. 'Do you know where he is?' she demanded.

Travis frowned. 'Isn't he in the barn?' As she shook her head, his frown deepened. 'He's probably hiding in the woods . . . or maybe he went in the cabin by the back door—I'll check there. Why don't you try the tool shed and the chicken house?'

With a lift of hope, Paige remembered that Brent always liked collecting the eggs. She hurried across the grass. The tool shed was empty, its tidiness a mockery, and the chicken house yielded only one roosting hen and three brown eggs. The kennels were also empty. Travis was just emerging from the back door; she turned her thumb down and headed for the alders that lay between the sheds and the river.

Ten minutes later she and Travis met by the river's edge. Paige forced herself to scan the rushing, ice-cold water, and said the obvious. 'You haven't found him.'

'No. I'm going to call Felix on the radio. Nell and the girls will keep an eye out around the house, and Felix can check the trail and the shore—he'll fire the rifle if Brent turns up. Then I'll head down to the dock with the dogs. You could check the woods around here.'

She nodded. Travis squeezed her shoulder. 'We'll find him, don't worry.'

Desperately needing his assurances, Paige muttered, 'If only we hadn't——'

'I know—I shouldn't have lost my temper,' he said harshly. 'I've learned something in the past few minutes, Paige. Stephanie's dead. But Brent's alive, and I owe him far more than I've been willing to give him.'

It was a huge admission, the change she had been waiting for. But Brent was not here to hear it. 'If he fell in the river, we'd never know,' she said in despair.

'I've warned him about the river, I don't think he'd go near it.'

Praying he was right, she said huskily, 'We'd better start looking.'

Travis gave her a smile which she knew was meant to be encouraging, even though it could not mask his anxiety. 'There's an old dinner gong hanging in the porch—if you find him, bang on it as hard as you can.' Then he whistled to the dogs and jogged up the hill.

Paige knew it was far more sensible that they split up. Yet, as she watched him go out of sight, a kind of primitive fear closed in on her. The whispering trees, the mountains, the sunlit sky, none of them cared whether Brent was found. Alive or dead made no difference to them. He was only one small boy . . .

Unable to bear the silence, she shouted his name, and to her overwrought imagination it seemed that the mountains threw it back to her in a mocking echo. Her palms were wet; she had never been this frightened in the back streets of San Francisco.

Stop this, Paige, she scolded herself. Think of Brent. Where would you go if you were he?

Not lingering by the river, she began beating her way through the woods, searching in an ever-widening circle around the cabin, her eyes peeled for any glimpse of a bright red T-shirt and a tousled brown head. She shouted until her voice was hoarse; she scaled rocks and criss-crossed the brook; branches whipped her face and snagged her clothing; her feet squelched in the bog near the river and mud splashed her legs. She was conscious of time passing and of an ever-burgeoning fear that she desperately tried to control, for it would not help Brent for her to sit down on the forest floor and have hysterics.

Then, as something crashed through the bushes, she thought for a heart-stopping moment that she had found him. But it was Minto who burst into the open, Chimo and Travis at his heels. 'Down, Minto,' she said automatically, and saw that Travis was alone.

'No sign of him?' he asked, his eyes searching her face.

'What will we do?' she whispered.

He put an arm around her, drawing her close, and for a moment Paige forgot all her worries in the comfort of being held. As she let her head rest on his shoulder, he traced a graze on her cheek. 'What did you do—walk into a tree?'

'It reached out and grabbed me,' she muttered. 'Felix hasn't fired the gun.'

'I think we should head that way . . . maybe Nell could relieve you for a while. If Brent hasn't turned up in the next hour, I'll radio the mainland and get a search party over here, we don't want him in the woods at night.'

He had verbalised her worst fear. 'I was the one who picked the fight with you,' she said miserably. 'It was my fault.'

'I was the one who told you to leave with Brent—I'd give

everything I own to be able to take those words back,' Travis answered roughly. His arm tightened. 'Come on, Paige, let's go to Nell's.' He glanced at the sky. 'The weather's going to break, too—another reason to find him as soon as possible.'

They followed the track to Felix's, taking occasional detours into the woods to call out Brent's name. When they reached the Camerons, the two girls were sitting disconsolately on the front porch. 'Did you find him?' Fiona called. Paige shook her head. 'Dad went up the inlet and Mum's looking in the woods out back. She told us to stay here in case he came, but we wanted to look too, didn't we, Beth?'

Beth had been crying. 'Why'd he get lost?' she wailed. 'I want to play with him.' Her woebegone blue eyes appealed to Paige for help. 'Maybe a bear's eaten him up.'

'Don't be silly,' her elder sister said crossly. 'Dad'll find him. Dad found me the day I fell in the creek.'

Paige picked Beth up. 'Fiona's right,' she said firmly. 'Your dad and Travis will find him. Let's go inside and get a cookie.'

Then Nell appeared on the track and Minto began to bark; she was alone, and when she saw the four of them by the porch her shoulders drooped and she looked very grave. 'Felix went along the shore of the inlet, Travis, and he was planning to double back on the trail.'

'I'll take the lakeshore, then. Perhaps you ought to go back to the cabin, Paige . . . he might just turn up there.'

Paige would have done anything to ease the terrible anxiety Travis was less and less able to conceal. 'All right, I will. Good luck.'

But as she put Beth down the crack of a rifle bullet sounded from the north, its echo reverberating in the hills. Paige clutched the child's hand so tightly that Beth yelped. Nell let out her breath in a long sigh. 'Thank God,' she said.

Travis leaned against the porch and covered his eyes with his hands; they were not quite steady, Paige saw, and felt her heart contract with pity. To deflect attention from him, she said loudly, 'Felix has found him. Fiona was right, Beth, your dad did find him.'

Beth's tears were forgotten. 'I knew he would,' she crowed.

'It was me who said so,' Fiona argued. 'How long before they get here, Mum?'

'Ten minutes or so,' Nell said knowledgeably. 'The shot wasn't that far away.'

Nine minutes later Felix came into sight on the track, carrying a small figure piggyback, his rifle slung barrel-down across his chest. Paige and Travis started off to meet him. But Paige lagged behind. This meeting, she sensed, should be between Travis and Brent, for Travis's decision had changed their roles; she was only a bit player now.

Felix was smiling. 'Found him up by Jake's Creek,' he said matter-of-factly. 'Didn't think he'd get that far. He's none the worse for wear . . . he and I had a little talk.'

'Thanks, Felix,' Travis said quietly. He walked around the other man and held out his arms.

Brent had twigs caught in his hair and his eyes were huge in his face, which was scratched to rival Paige's. He gulped audibly. 'I shouldn't've run away,' he said.

Travis swung him into his arms. 'I made a very bad mistake too, Brent—I didn't think I wanted you to live with me. But I've changed my mind and I'd really like you to stay with me. If you want to.'

He had not needed to add that last phrase, thought Paige, for what real choice did Brent have? She found herself waiting with bated breath for the boy's reply.

Brent scowled in thought, looking very much like the man who was holding him. 'You won't yell at Paige any more?'

Travis winced. 'No.'

'Can I still play with Beth 'n' Fiona?'

'Yes.'

Brent's smile was like a sunburst. 'OK,' he chirped. 'I'll stay.'

Briefly Travis rested his cheek on the boy's curls and closed his eyes; he had not been at all sure of Brent's decision, Paige realised, and wished she could burst into tears to get rid of some of the emotion that was clogging her throat. Felix winked at her and she blinked hard. Then she heard Travis say, 'I've never been a father before, Brent, so I've got a lot to learn. But I promise I'll do the best I can.'

'C'n I have a cookie?' said Brent.

Felix cleared his throat. 'Of course you can. I reckon the rest of us deserve something a little stronger, wouldn't you agree, Travis?'

The four adults toasted Brent's return in home-made elderberry wine that slid deliciously down Paige's throat and then exploded into liquid fire inside her. 'No more,' she said hastily when Nell offered her a second helping. 'Not if I'm expected to walk home.'

'It would be a challenge to carry both of you,' Travis said lazily. He was stretched out on the couch, his long body relaxed. Paige looked away before her face could betray her, for clearly in her mind was the image of that same body stretched out naked beside hers on the grass. The hand holding his glass had cupped her breast; his thigh had been thrown over her hip. She drained the last of the elderberry wine, and for at least the third time that day wished she could burst into tears.

CHAPTER FIVE

WITH a minimum of fuss, Nell produced a late supper of burgers, salad and stawberries from her garden. When the dishes were cleared away, Travis said, 'Time to go, Brent, it'll soon be dark.'

'I don't want to go yet, I want to play with Beth,' Brent said fretfully.

'Bedtime,' Travis said, and picked him up. 'You can play here tomorrow.'

In two sentences he had established his authority, Paige thought wryly, and stood up herself. Her whole body felt numb, whether from elderberry wine or exhaustion she could not have said. The trip home—and she now thought of it as home—was accomplished largely in silence; Brent frankly asleep, Paige and Travis busy with their own thoughts.

Paige took off her sneakers in the porch, then held Brent while Travis unlaced his boots. 'I'll undress him,' Travis said. 'Do you mind lighting the lamp and then heating a bit of water? I suppose we should wash his face.'

She did mind, although she had no right to. It was important for Travis to establish a relationship with Brent as quickly as possible, and for her to feel jealous was petty and foolish; or so she told herself as she pumped some water into the kettle and set it on the stove. Then she went into the bedroom to get Brent's pyjamas.

When she came back, Travis had taken off the boy's red shirt and the jeans that now looked as though Brent had lived in them for at least a month. The boy was awake, his violet eyes heavy-lidded in his scratched face. He gave Paige a sleepy smile which she managed to respond to quite naturally.

The chill had gone from the water, so she poured some into the basin and put it on the table beside Brent. With infinite gentleness Travis washed the boy's face. Then he put on the pyjama jacket, buttoning it carefully, and reached down to pull off Brent's socks. Brent must have travelled through a bog that day; the socks, originally red, were now black, and smelled richly of peat. Travis took the first one by the cuff and eased it over the boy's foot, wrinkling his nose. Then suddenly his face changed and his whole body stilled.

'What's wrong?' Paige asked, puzzled.

'His little toe—has it always been that way?'

'Bent in, you mean? Yes . . . the other one's the same, apparently he was born that way. It's no big deal, Travis.' The last thing she wanted was Brent to become self-conscious about so small a matter.

Travis looked over at her, his face blank with shock and drained of its natural colour. 'Mine are the same,' he said.

Paige frowned at him, her brain grappling with the significance of his statement. 'You mean . . . it's hereditary?'

'That's exactly what I mean. My father and my grand-father had the same thing. A dominant gene, the family doctor said. Nothing to worry about . . . why didn't you *tell* me, Paige?'

She said defensively, 'It didn't seem important. Anyway, I didn't realise yours were the same.' Today, when she had seen Travis naked, her mind had not been on his feet, she thought with painful honesty, and felt her cheeks grow hot.

But Travis was following his own train of thought, his words tumbling over one another. 'You see what this means? Brent *is* my son. Stephanie lied to me. She was carrying *my* child when she left me. Once he was born, she would have known the significance of Brent's toes . . . but she never bothered to let me know. She never told me that I had a son.'

The protective sheen had gone from his eyes, their depths full of an intense anguish. 'Five lost years,' he muttered. 'Why didn't she tell me? She had her faults, God knows, but she wasn't intentionally malicious or cruel.'

'The man she ran away with . . . perhaps she'd told him she was pregnant by him. Then, when it became apparent Brent wasn't his son, she was too proud to admit her mistake.'

Travis gave his head a little shake. 'She's dead now, so I suppose I'll never know.' He rested his big hands on Brent's shoulders as if he were holding something infinitely precious; the boy looked confused and frightened. 'Brent, it's all right,' he said softly. 'Maybe you won't understand this—but I have the same toes that you do.' He grinned. 'Heading the wrong way, my grandfather always used to say. East-west instead of north-south. You see, that proves that I'm your father. Your real father. Before you were born I was told you weren't, and I believed that. So when you came here with Paige I didn't think you could be my son, and I was angry when she argued with me. But now I know you are.'

Brent still looked bewildered. 'Not an uncle?'

'No. A real father. If you ever have a son, he'll have funny toes too.'

Brent stared at his feet. 'They're dirty,' he said helpfully.

Travis picked him up and hugged him to his chest; there were tears shining in his eyes. 'You're my son,' he said huskily. 'My dearly beloved son . . .'

Paige turned away, for the scene was private and she an interloper. She was happy for Brent, truly she was. Why, then, did she feel as if the whole world had been snatched from her, leaving her confronting a yawning abyss?

She said overloudly, 'I'll turn down the bed,' and fled up the stairs. She must hold back her tears another few minutes until she was alone. She had to. Stripping off her clothes, she dragged on her nightgown, which was peach-coloured with an empire waist and capped sleeves, covering her quite adequately. Then she sat on the bed to wait.

The door opened and Travis came in carrying Brent, who had fallen asleep. He walked around the far side of the bed and put the child down, pulling the covers over him with a tenderness that cut Paige to the heart. She said, and again her voice sounded overloud, 'You should sleep here—I'll sleep on the couch.' She scrambled to her feet.

The lamplight from the living-room shone through the folds of her gown. Travis said in a strange voice, 'No. The whole situation's new to him—you stay with him as you always have . . . As soon as I can get the materials, I'll build on a room for him.'

Quickly she got into bed, almost as though she needed Brent for protection, although whether from Travis or from herself she could not have said. 'Goodnight,' she mumbled.

He came round the end of the bed and sat down on the duvet. 'I know you're tired, Paige, but there's something I have to say.'

He wanted her to stay here and help him look after Brent . . . the hope was like a shaft of sunlight, piercing the darkness of the forest.

'I owe you a great deal,' Travis said heavily. 'You would have been perfectly justified in leaving here with Brent that very first day . . . I didn't exactly encourage you to stay, did I? In fact, I was extremely rude to you. But you did stay, for Brent's sake. And now it's all worked out and I've been given the gift of a son I didn't even know existed . . . Thank you, Paige.' He gave her a grave smile. 'I'll always be grateful to you.'

Perhaps later, when she was back in San Francisco, she

would be able to recall these words with pleasure. But now Paige felt heartsick. Only wanting him to be gone, she muttered, 'I stayed because I had to. There was nowhere else to take him.'

'You stayed because you have principles you believe in, and because you cared what happened to a small boy who essentially was no concern of yours,' Travis contradicted her gently. Then he stood up. 'I'll let you get to sleep. Don't feel you have to get up early in the morning, I'll take care of Brent. Goodnight, Paige.'

He left the room, pulling the door shut behind him, so she was enveloped in darkness. She lay back on the pillows, scarcely aware of Brent's quiet breathing beside her, and let the tears flow down her cheeks.

When Paige woke up the next morning, she was alone in the room and the cabin was quiet. Ordinarily she would have leaped out of bed and gone in search of Brent; but today she did not have to. Travis would be looking after Brent. She was redundant.

She lay still. She could hear the wind in the trees, and raindrops were trickling down the window-pane. They looked like tears. She remembered Brent crying as he'd pounded his fists against Travis's leg. She remembered the sheen of tears in Travis's eyes when he had gathered his son into his arms. She remembered her own silent weeping last night. Too many tears for one day, she thought miserably. But then, far too much had happened yesterday.

Watching the rivulets of water course down the glass, she wondered if she and Travis would have made love yesterday if it had been raining. Probably not. There would have been nowhere for them to go. Yet to have her fate dependent on such a chance occurrence as the weather seemed both unfair and unacceptable. Was she just a puppet, whose strings had been pulled by a few hours of sunlight and a man's random appearance on the shores of a lake?

Paige turned over, trying to find a comfortable place in the pillow. If only they hadn't made love! Had it not been for that, she could have faced Travis's acceptance of Brent and her own inevitable departure with some degree of equanimity.

Everything had worked out far better for Brent than she had anticipated. Travis would be a good father, combining firmness with love, while Nell, Fiona and Beth would provide the softening influences of femininity; and the wilderness would teach him self-reliance. Brent would be happy.

But she would miss him, she knew. She had grown fond of him.

A pine bough was scraping against the roof. She listened to it, thinking how lonely a sound it was, like a dead soul seeking entrance. She was not being honest with herself. She was much more than fond of Brent. She loved him.

I should have stayed in San Francisco. There I know the rules. There I keep my distance from the boys, even the ones like Pedro. But here I relaxed my guard, and I didn't notice what was happening until it was too late. I'm going to hate leaving Brent. It will be like leaving a piece of myself behind.

Which led her inexorably to Travis. How was she to get in his boat today and go across the lake and say a calm good-bye to him on the wooden dock? Nelson's Landing and San Francisco were separated by more than geographical distance; she was under no illusions that Travis would seek her out in San Franscisco. When she left here, she would never see him again.

The thought filled her with anguish. Because he walked with the grace of a wild creature and his hair shone like a raven's wing? Because his eyes so rarely revealed their secrets that she was drawn to penetrate their depths? Because he made love with passion and intelligence and generosity?

I'm falling in love with him, she thought, panic-stricken.

She couldn't do that. She had a life in a faraway city, a job with people who depended on her, and a circle of friends She also had a brother's grave to tend.

She had not thought a great deal about Martie lately. The cords that bound her to him, invisible and powerful, seemed to have loosened here, so that she was no longer driven by the compulsions his death had engendered. Nor had she given much thought to her job, she realised with a pang of guilt. How was Brit doing with his new foster parents? Had Sandy finally been sent to a home for delinquents? And what about Pedro? Pedro was an inveterate and highly skilful shoplifter, with big black eyes that could swim with repentance, and a tongue as smooth as honey. She, Paige, now saw through him. But the new caseworker would not . . . How could she have allowed Teko Bay to have driven all the concerns of her job out of her mind?

Not Teko Bay, she thought. Travis. Travis was the one who had driven Martie and her buried grief and her compulsive working habits from her mind. Travis was the key to the way she was feeling. He was the reason, more than any other, why she must leave Teko Bay. Because she was in danger of falling in love with him, however far-fetched that might seem, and, for her own sake, the sooner she left here, the better. There could be no future in it. Her life and his were worlds apart. Anyway, she added with incorrigible honesty, Travis had given no indication that the feeling was in any way mutual.

Travis had wanted to make love to her, he had made no secret of that. And with her full co-operation he had achieved his aim. After which, he could not wait to get rid of her, she thought cynically. Oh, he had dressed it up in a lot of high-sounding words. But essentially her continued presence here would be a source of embarrassment. He did not want an affair with her, he had made that clear, and certainly he did not want to marry her. Her departure today would no doubt be a great relief.

Wishing that her conclusions did not make her feel so wretchedly unhappy, she realised the rain had abated. Fewer tears, she thought with a twist of her mouth. Keep that in mind. And always remember that Travis is too much of a gentleman to ask you to leave now that he's in your debt—he would never be that churlish. It's up to you to make the move.

She heard the thud of boots in the porch and Brent's high-pitched chatter mixed with Travis's deeper tones. All her tidy rationalisations dropped away as she was swamped in a great wave of pain, tossed and tumbled like a piece of driftwood. I don't want to leave, she thought frantically. I can't bear to leave. But I have to.

She heard Travis and Brent go outside again. With the air of a woman going to her own execution, Paige got out of bed and she began to pack. It did not take long. She neatly folded Nell's smock, knowing with a fresh stab of pain that she would have to say goodbye to the Camerons. How had she managed to put down such a deep roots in so short a time?

Putting her case in the living-room, with Nell's clothes on a nearby chair, Paige then forced herself to eat something. She was rinsing out the cereal bowl when she heard the outer door open again. Every nerve in her body tightened unbear-ably. Her spoon clattered to the floor.

'Do I have to come in?' Brent was complaining.

'Yes. I don't want you getting wet through. You can go out later on.'

Brent clumped into the room, his expression as gloomy as the water. 'C'n I go to Beth's, then?'

'Later,' Travis said patiently. He smiled at Paige. 'The after-effects of yesterday are very much in evidence,' he added.

'The joys of fatherhood,' she answered lightly. 'I could take Brent over to the Camerons, I have to go there to say goodbye.'

Travis's eyes narrowed. 'What do you mean?'

'I'm leaving,' she said with rather overdone forbearance. 'We talked about it yesterday, remember?'

'You're not leaving today.'

She had not expected him to argue. With an effort that was almost physical, she subdued a flicker of hope. 'I have to, Travis. My vacation's running out, and you don't need me here any more.' She produced a creditable smile. 'I can go home to the firm of lawyers and tell them I've accomplished all that was required.'

'Paige,' Travis said, 'I'm afraid the lawyers will have to wait for that admirable little speech. You're not going home today, and I rather doubt you'll be going for the next three or four days. Have you looked out of the window?'

She stared at him. 'It's raining. So what?'

'The rain's nothing. But the wind on the lake is between forty and fifty knots, and I happen to be averse to death by drowning. You're staying put.'

'Felix will take me!'

'Don't you understand what I'm saying? No one in Teko Bay or Nelson's Landing would put a boat on that lake today.'

'But I've *got* to go home!'

'You can't, he said shortly.

Brent faltered, 'What's wrong, Paige?'

Travis added meaningfully, 'So take off your jacket and put your case back in the room . . . we agreed no more shouting matches in front of Brent, right?'

Boiling with frustration, Paige gave him a look that should have shrivelled him. 'Then perhaps,' she suggested, 'you could give Brent his breakfast and you and I could continue this discussion outside.'

'There's nothing more to discuss.'

'I happen to disagree.'

He returned her look with one of his own; but anger was forging through Paige's veins, and she merely tilted her chin defiantly, her cheeks pink with temper. Athough she was quite sure he wanted to shake her like a puppy, she was equally sure he would not do it.

He said, for their ears alone, 'You look even more beautiful right now than you did when we made love.'

Her nostrils flared. But she said dulcetly, 'That's called hitting below the belt.'

He smothered a laugh. 'Stephanie was never a fighter. You do make life interesting, Paige.'

To find herself liking him would make it twice as difficult to leave. She said icily, 'I'll wait for you outside.'

He grinned. 'Put on some raingear, won't you?'

Conquering urges to stamp her feet, tear out her hair and slam the door, Paige went into the porch and hauled on the jacket Nell had loaned her. Then she stepped outside. The clouds were piled higher than the mountains, their edges ragged and torn, while the wind tugged at her hair and cooled her flushed cheeks, so that momentarily she was grateful for its wildness and vigour, so close to her own mood. The cabin had muffled the sounds of the storm. Rain was gurgling in the gutters and dripping from the eaves; the oak leaves argued among themselves and the pine boughs sighed their distress.

When she had been lying in bed that morning, Paige had been thinking of the people she would miss in Teko Bay. Now she realised she would miss more than the people, for the log cabin, set against the mountains and surrounded by trees and water, had also claimed a place in her heart. Despite all that had happened, she had found a peace and inner contentment here that the city had never given her; perhaps, she thought, that was why she had put down so many roots so quickly, her instincts recognising that the place was right for her. That in some strange way she belonged.

I have to leave, she thought with the calmness of despair. The longer I stay, the harder it will be to go.

As if on cue, Travis stepped outside. Before she could say anything, he remarked inconsequentially, 'Your hair is redder when it's wet.'

She did not want him making comments on her person; he had forfeited that right. Vowing to keep her temper, she pleaded, 'Travis, is there seriously no way I can get across the lake today? Surely someone in the village has a bigger boat? I don't care what it costs . . . I just have to get out of here.'

'So were you fooling me yesterday?' he askd tightly. 'Was what happened so awful that you can't wait to leave?'

Her answer was purposely evasive. 'You and Brent settled your differences yesterday, so there's no reason for me to stay.'

He took her by the elbow. 'You can't stand the sight of me, is that what you're trying to say?'

'You're exaggerating,' Paige replied coolly. 'There's no need for melodrama. We're two adults who happened to have made love yesterday, which under the circumstances was scarcely surprising——'

'Nell's very pretty sister was here all last summer, and I didn't want to make love to her.'

'So maybe you have a thing for redheads,' she said fliply. 'The point is we both decided it shouldn't happen again. I personally find the situation a little awkward——'

'Awkward?' he exploded. 'That's a hell of a word to use.'

'It's a perfectly good word. Frankly, I think it would have been better if we hadn't made love.' There. She had finally said something that was the truth. 'However, I accept full, responsibility for my part in——'

'For heaven's sake, you sound like the village school-marm—come off it, Paige! Don't pretend to be cold-blooded and calculating with me. I, of all people, know better.'

Her hands were balled into fists; she thrust them into her pockets and snapped, 'Oddly enough, I do have concerns other than you, Travis Renshaw. I have a job that I'm supposed to report to in four days—do you want me to get fired?'

'Tell the truth, you're wedded to that damned job,' he snarled. 'I saw the state you were in when you arrived here . . . might be the best thing in the world if you did get fired.'

She forgot her vow in a surge of fury, perhaps because at some level she suspected he was telling the truth. 'Some of us have our living to earn! It's too bad you don't have to do the same. There's nothing like having to pay the bills to give you a bit of incentive. If you hadn't made so much on that first book, you'd have been forced into writing more.'

His hand tightened cruelly around her sleeve. 'It's not like that—I *can't* write,' he said hoarsely.

'When did you last try?'

He was silent, his face a taut mask, so that her temper died as quickly as it had arisen. She ran her fingers through her damp hair. 'I'm sorry, I shouldn't have said that.'

'You despise me, don't you?' he interjected. 'A sex-starved layabout, that's how you see me.'

'Who's hurting my arm,' she replied. As he dropped her sleeve with an incoherent exclamation, she met his gaze, her brown eyes lambent with truth. 'No, I don't see you that way at all, Travis. I just don't believe you're a one-book writer. You're too intelligent and subtle. You're too full of passion.' She risked a little smile. 'Which I, of all people, should know . . . But five years ago, I suppose because of what happened with Stephanie, you fell into the Hollywood trap and associated yourself with two extremely bad movies. And perhaps a life-style to match, I don't know. You were right to feel guilty for what you did . . . I know that because I read your book, so I know how badly you undersold yourself. But you can't allow guilt to stifle you forever. That was five years ago, Travis, and if this place hasn't cleaned your soul, nowhere will.'

She had run out of words. Although she was rather horrified by her temerity, she had no intention of taking anything back; all she prayed was that he make no remarks about busybody social workers. He said slowly. 'How do you know all that?'

She shrugged helplessly. 'Is it true?'

'I wanted to show her!' he said violently. 'That I could make just as much money as her lovers and spend it as quickly, too. That I could make the headlines in the gossip papers, and attract beautiful women . . . It all sounds pretty childish now, I know. But remember that I'd just surfaced from spending nearly six years on a book I'd doubted would even be published.'

'Did you neglect Stephanie during those years?' Paige asked quietly.

He nodded, unsurprised by her question. 'I thought she was happy. I thought we were enough in love that things like money and parties weren't particularly important. I was wrong on both counts.'

A raindrop trickled down Paige's neck, and she shivered. If she had been honest with Travis, he had been equally honest in return, exposing his blindness to her, and his faults. Becoming a real person, she thought, and shivered again. She was supposed to be fleeing from Travis. Not growing closer to him. 'Do you still love her?' she heard herself say.

His surprise had to be genuine. 'Of course not. Why do you ask?'

She shifted uncomfortably. 'I thought perhaps you did.'

'I told you once before that that chapter in my life was closed, Paige.'

And he was not ready or willing to start a new one . . . She said with a gaucheness unusual to her, 'Travis, are you sure about that boat?'

Her question jarred him back to the present. 'Yes, I'm sure,' he rasped. 'No one within a hundred miles of here would go out on the lake today.'

'But it doesn't seem that windy!'

'Paige, the cabin was built on the most sheltered location on the peninsula. Go down to the dock if you don't believe me.'

She stamped her foot, an action that gave her immense satisfaction, even while she lamented its immaturity. 'All right, I will. I *can't* stay here another three or four days!'

'One thing you haven't yet learned about Teko Bay—the weather controls you, not the reverse. And all the foot-stamping in the world won't change that.' Without altering his voice, he added, 'When you scowl at me like that, I have the strongest urge to take you in my arms and kiss the fight right out of you.'

Paige took two steps backward, her cheeks paling. 'No—no, you mustn't!'

There was no mistaking her sincerity. 'Oh, don't worry,' he said viciously. 'I'll stay out of your way the next three days. Starting right now.' Pivoting, he pulled open the porch door and disappeared inside. He did not shut the door; he slammed it.

Paige cringed at the noise. Although her blue cotton trousers were wet through and her hair plastered to her face, and although a walk to the dock was less than appealing, her pride insisted that she carry it through. Keeping her hands in her pockets, Paige set off down the track.

As she tramped along, the wind gathered force, lashing the trees into a frenzy, the branches creaking like the rigging of a ship in a gale; she heard the lake before she saw it, the thud and tumble of the waves on the shore as if an animal were caught in a trap and roaring out its pain and fury. But even that did not quite prepare her for the sight.

Her first thought was that Travis had been telling the truth; her second that nothing on God's earth would entice her on to the lake today. The village was invisible through torn veils of spray that seemed to merge with the scudding grey clouds, and she would have been willing to swear that the ground was shaking from the impact of the waves.

The excesses of nature had always tended to exhilarate Paige rather than frighten her. Today, however, was different. The stretch of storm-tossed water between her and the village was as effective as a prison wall built of stone and capped with barbed wire. She was a captive in Teko Bay. Against every instinct in her body, she had to stay here.'

CHAPTER SIX

'WHY are you sleeping? It's daytime!'

Brent was bouncing on the duvet. Paige opened one eye. After her abortive trip to the dock, she had walked home to find the cabin deserted, Travis and Brent presumably having gone to the Camerons'. She had hung her wet clothes around the wood stove, climbed into bed, and fallen asleep.

Now she grabbed at Brent's leg. He shrieked with laughter and plumped himself on top of her, trying to pull the covers off her shoulders.

From the doorway, Travis said repressively, 'Don't bother Paige, Brent—she's trying to sleep.'

In a flash of insight, Paige realised Travis did not want Brent getting any more attached to her than he already was; a very sensible attitude that cut her to the quick. She said with a lightness that almost succeeded, 'Go with your father, Brent. I'm going to get up.'

'I got a puzzle from Fiona. Play with me?'

Feeling her heart twist, she replied, 'I'm going for a walk when I get up. Maybe later,' and saw perplexity cloud the violet eyes. Three days was already beginning to seem like a life sentence.

This time Paige dressed in jeans and a warmer sweater, and made her escape outdoors. Travis, she noticed, made no attempt to stop her. She strode along the track towards the Camerons, finding a kind of release in the exercise; but before she got to their house she took a trail that branched off to the right and circled behind the house, bisecting the peninsula that separated the lake from the inlet. It was the trail Travis must have taken the day he'd discovered her by the shore and made love to her. Yesterday, she thought with a dull surprise. It felt like a lifetime ago.

Paige trudged on, trying not to think, knowing she must tire herself enough to sleep that night. The wind was stronger now because she was on the crest of the ridge, and the sky was so overcast that it was almost dark under the trees; had she not been so sunk in misery, she might have been frightened.

She was never sure what it was that alerted her. A hint of movement through the trees? A sense that she was no longer alone? It could not have been a sound for the wind drowned out all but its own cacophony. She looked up sharply, stopping in her tracks.

For a moment she saw nothing, and started to chide herself for an overactive imagination. Then her heart skipped a beat. Something had moved near that giant pine tree. She could not see what it was. But it had been real, not imaginary.

She held her ground, her pulse racing, for Travis had warned her not to run from a bear. But then a shadow moved between two rocks to her right, and another slunk from behind a beech tree. The shape near the giant pine vanished, reappearing closer to her. Wolves, she thought, and felt her mouth go dry.

She had mistaken Chimo and Minto for wolves on her first evening in Teko Bay, she told herself stoutly. These must be dogs as well . . . But whose?

Something rustled behind her. She whirled. The animal was only fifteen feet from her, so close she could see the individual whiskers on the long grey muzzle, and its yellow eyes, startlingly intelligent. It did not look like a husky.

She was surrounded.

Then another noise overrode the cry of the wind. Heavier steps than those of the wolves. Her heart hammering in her ears, Paige turned to face this new threat, and with a sense of incredulity saw a gnome-like figure, bent and wrinkled, materialise from the shadowed forest and head towards her. Nightmare turned to farce, for the old man was a character not from Stephen King, but from Walt Disney. He was bearded and grizzled, his panhandler's hat, wide braces and leather lace-up boots from another generation. She said in a cracked voice, 'Are those wolves?'

She had startled him, and took courage from the fact that he looked more frightened than she. He sat down on a stump several feet away from her, his bushy brows meeting across his nose. After a period of thought, he said, 'No.'

'I saw them!' she cried indignantly.

He jumped at the sharpness of her tone. Suddenly afraid that he would melt into the woods as mysteriously as he had appeared, she said more gently, 'I'm sorry, I didn't mean to yell. But look over there—aren't those wolves?'

'Dogs' he said.

'Your dogs?'

He seemed to find her question rhetorical. He also looked a little less wary of her, she decided and said casually, 'My name's Paige.' The dogs were now arrayed behind him, four of them, as similar to wolves as anything she was ever likely to see.

No response. 'I'm staying with Travis Renshaw,' she added.

His cogitations took longer this time. 'You his wife?'

She was not sure if he was interested in her identity, or concerned about her morals. 'No. I brought his son here from San Francisco.'

She had his full attention now. 'Son?'

'His wife died recently, and Travis has guardianship of their child.'

'Well.'

It seemed as good a comment as any. Paige took two steps

towards him, curious to see him more closely. One of the dogs growled. She stopped and said persuasively, 'You haven't told me anything about yourself.'

'Don't talk much.'

She hid a smile and sat down on the wet ground, sensing that made him less nervous. 'Aren't you a prospector? I looked for gold in the creek, but I didn't find any.'

'None there.'

'Do your dogs have names?'

'Never bothered naming them. Used to have a whole team. Only four left now.'

It was by far his longest speech. 'Do tell me your name,' she coaxed, and saw with a thrill of superstitious fear that his eyes were the same colour as those of the dogs.

'Theo. Theo Herrick.'

He said the words like a talisman, as if only his name preserved his identity; with a sharp pang of pity, she wondered how long it was since he had spoken to another human being. 'Do you live near here?'

He gestured behind him. 'Up that way.'

An answer that covered a lot of territory, she thought drily. 'If I don't go home tomorrow, may I come and visit you?' Surely Felix would know where he lived.

The old man stood up so suddenly that she was startled. Like puppets, the four dogs stood too. 'Know your way home?' Theo asked gruffly.

'Yes. But——'

With a gesture that was rusty with disuse, he touched his hand to his hat brim, and then, at an awkward lope, vanished among the trees—the dogs, silent as wolves, at his heels.

Paige stood up, wiping the pine needles from her jacket. That certainly had to be one of the strangest conversations she had ever had in her life. If it even qualified as a conversation. Deep in thought and oblivious to the rain, she marched back along the trail to the Camerons.

Nell was making one of her famous soups, for which no recipe could possibly exist. Paige hung up her coat and said unceremoniously, 'I met the most peculiar old man in the woods. He said his name was Theo Herrick.'

Nell put down the carrot she was peeling. 'You mean, he told you his name?'

Paige grinned. 'It took a while.'

'He won't even talk to me. Runs away like a rabbit. What have you got that I haven't?'

'Persistence? Tell me about him, Nell.'

Nell passed her the vegetable peeler and some more carrots. 'He and his older brother came out from England in the twenties to take up prospecting. From what I've heard they were never very sociable. They built a cabin four miles from here and roamed the hills looking for gold, years after year, just the two of them. The brother died seven months ago, so Theo's alone now . . . Travis keeps an eye on him, taking him supplies, and fresh vegetables in the summer. For some reason he trusts Travis. I shouldn't think he's talked to a woman in years.'

'I'm flattered.' With some gusto, Paige related the appearance of the so-called wolves. 'If I'm still here tomorrow, I think I'll try and visit him.'

'What do you mean, if you're still here? You're not leaving?' Nell asked in dismay. 'Travis told us the good news this morning about Brent being his son. But that doesn't mean you have to leave.'

'I've got to be at work on Monday, Nell.'

Look uncharacteristically flustered, Nell exclaimed, 'I was really hoping that you and Travis——'

'Not a chance,' Paige interrupted ruthlessly. 'And I'm getting too found of Brent, Nell. It's better I go.'

Clasping a turnip in front of her like a votive offering, Nell said, 'I'll miss you. We'll all miss you . . . I don't know what's the matter with Travis.' She scowled at the turnip as if it were his head she was holding.

Paige did not want to discuss Travis's shortcomings. She had found out something else about him today, that he cared enough for a lonely old man to trek four miles through the woods with food; and, of course, with companionship. It would be so much easier to leave Travis if only she could legitmately despise him.

She passed Nell half a dozen peeled carrots. 'Shall I chop the celery?'

Nell was still hugging the turnip. 'He needs a woman,' she said.

Nell was normally the soul of discretion. 'So does Theo,' Paige said flippantly, and wrested the turnip from Nell's grasp. 'Here, let me do that.'

'Are you sure you're not the smallest bit in love with him?'

Paige sliced the turnip in half with one vicious swipe of the cleaver. 'No!' Picking up the vegetable knife, she began hacking at the skin.

'Careful, you're wasting it,' Nell said. 'I don't care what you say, Paige—I'm going to hope this wind lasts for at least a week. And now we'll talk about something else.'

Which they did, until Paige left for home an hour later. In the cabin Travis was frying fishcakes on the stove, and Brent was shelling peas, his face screwed up in concentration. The two of them looked entirely self-sufficient, Paige thought dismally, and began to set the table. A week after she was gone Brent would probably have forgotten her, and she was not sure whether Travis would miss her at all. For some reason, she did not tell him about her meeting with Theo.

However, once Brent was in bed she said to Travis, 'I'd better get in touch with my friend Barbara, to let her know I probably won't be back at work on time.'

'I'll put the call through for you—might be quite a bit of static because of the weather. Give me her number in San

Francisco.' Then he flicked on the radio set and picked up the microphone. 'North Mountain channel, 3W-7935, calling Yukon operator. North Mountain channel, 3W-7935, calling Yukon operator. Over.'

'Yukon operator. Go ahead, North Mountain. How're you doing, Travis? Over.'

'Not bad, Sadie. Can you get me a number in San Francisco?' He gave the details, and for a few seconds there was only the crackling of static on the line while the connection was made. Then, miraculously, Paige heard Barbara's voice. 'Hello?'

'Call for you from Teko Bay, dear,' Sadie said. 'You can't talk while the other party's talking, got that? Over.'

Travis passed Paige the mike. She seized it and said eagerly, 'Barbara? It's Paige. How are you? Listen, I'm stuck up here, I can't get out for three or four days because of the weather—will you give Mrs Solvero a call and ask for a couple of days' extension on my leave? Over.' Mrs Solvero was her boss, and fortunately a very reasonable woman.

Barbara was in full spate. ' . . . already did, isn't that lucky? How's the famous author? Has he finally figured out that the boy just might be his son, or is he still into denial?'

Horribly aware of Travis sitting not three feet from her, Paige said strongly, 'Barb, I can't hear you when I'm talking. But half of northern B.C. and the Yukon can hear you—it's a radio-phone, not a regular phone . . . What do you mean, you already did? Did what? And have you heard anything of any of the boys? Now, once I say "over", it's your turn. Over.'

Sounding a touch chastened, Barbara said, 'Sorry. The boys are all fine, doing very well without you, difficult though that is to believe, and your replacement only took three days to cotton on to Pedro. So that front's covered. I was absolutely delighted when you didn't come home on the first dog sled, Paige darling, and even more delighted when you told me you were surrounded by mountains—mountains can have a very salutary effect on one's view of the world. A dozen ranges between you and your job wouldn't be one too many. So I took it upon myself to have a heart-to-heart with Mrs Solvero, and your vacation's extended another two weeks. More if you need it.' She continued insouciantly, 'Maybe I'd better chatter on for a few more minutes to let you get used to the idea. I wouldn't want your response to shock any of your Yukon listeners. Social services owe you every bit of that vacation, Paige. You've put in tons of overtime, and it's too bad there couldn't be a three-week hurricane, if that's what it takes to keep you there. Have you calmed down? Chewed your fingernails to the elbow? Your turn to talk now—but do remember your audience. Over to you!'

'How could you *do* that?' Paige yelped. 'Over.'

'Why don't you just call me an interfering bitch and be done with it? I also cancelled your rental car. Over.'

'Barbara, extending my vacation is not going to keep me here. I told you I want time in my apartment . . . I'm coming home as soon as I can. Over.'

'San Francisco weather's at its absolute worst, darling, smog and fog, any hurricane would be preferable to this. How's Eustace Percival Brent Renshaw? Over.'

'He's settling in extremely well with his father and I'm no longer needed here. I'll be home in less than a week.' Read between the lines, Barbara, she thought desperately. Am I supposed to say I'm falling in love with the father and I already love the son, when said father is sitting so close to me that I can hear him breathing? 'Over,' she said.

Barbara's forcefulness conquered all the wheezings and hisses on the line. 'Stay, Paige,' she said. 'For the good of your soul, stay.' With a loud click, she cut off the connection.

'Finished, dear?' Sadie asked cheerfully. 'Yukon operator to North Mountain channel, over and out.'

Paige put down the microphone with excessive care, avoiding Travis's eyes. She said bitterly, 'When you've got friends like that, who needs enemies?'

As he reached across her to switch off the radio, she caught the scent of his skin, agonisingly familiar, so that she almost missed what he was saying. 'I should think she's a very good friend. She's certainly keen to keep several hundred miles between you and your job.'

'I love my job! I wish everyone would stop treating it like some kind of monster that's devouring me for breakfast!'

'Good simile. You had a rather cadaverous look when you got here.' Suddenly he laughed. 'Say it, Paige—or else go outside and chop a couple of blocks of wood and put all that pent-up emotion to good use.'

'Surely it's repressed sexuality,' she said nastily.

'We could put that to even better use.'

'If you were smart, you wouldn't be suggesting I go any-where near an axe right now.'

'How very bloodthirsty you sound,' he murmured, and leaned forward. 'Your eyes have tiny flecks of gold in them . . . I noticed that when we were making love.'

She glowered at him, determined not to respond to the laughter still lurking in his eyes. 'Fool's gold.'

He tilted his chair back against the wall, folding his arms across his chest. 'I seem to be embroiled in a moral dilemma. The upright citizen in me says no affair. But the baser man would like nothing better than very thoroughly to seduce you, Paige.'

By an immense effort of will, she kept her poise. 'There's no dilemma,' she said sweetly. 'Just a two-letter, one-syllable word. No.'

'Maybe during this week-long hurricane of Barbara's you'll change your mind,' Travis said, and the look in his eyes made a frisson travel the length of her spine. Then he straightened. 'I'm going to read for a while. What about you?'

The book wasn't written that could hold her attention tonight. 'I think I'll go to bed,' Paige said, and knew that both of them recognised this as a blatant retreat. 'I'll see you in the morning.'

'Goodnight, Paige,' he said with imperturbable courtesy. 'Sleep well.'

Paige did *not* sleep well. She tucked herself into bed beside Brent, and for almost an hour perused an astonishingly dull book about the gold rush in Nelson's Landing, a book she had been convinced would put her to sleep in five minutes. She tried to understand the difference between hydraulic mining, dredging and quartz-mining, she loaded her brain with statistics, and dates, and all the while at another level of her consciousness she was aware of every sound from the other room. Eventually she turned off the lamp and composed herself for sleep.

She was first too warm and then too cold. The mattress had developed lumps that would have put the princess's pea to shame, while the pillows defeated every attempt to pound them into submission. Brent muttered in his sleep. The wind keened through the trees. The wind that had made her a captive in this place against her will . . . She dreamed of bears wearing braces and of gold nuggets tumbling down cliff faces, to be sorted out and carefully counted by Barbara, who was gripping a quill pen and looking quite delightful in a flat-brimmed stetson. One of the nuggets had landed on someone's foot. He was groaning . . .

Paige woke up with a jump. Someone had groaned. She would swear it. She stretched out an arm, but Brent was peacefully sleeping.

The light was still on in the other room. She lay tense, and heard a sound like paper being torn. Then again she heard that muffled groan.

Thoroughly alarmed, she climbed out of bed and padded on bare feet to the door. Edging it open, she peered around it. Travis was sitting at the pine table, his body slumped over a typewriter, his head buried in his arms. Her first impulse was to close the door and go to bed, for his attitude was one of complete defeat, and as such surely private. But the long curve of his backbone and the tousled head aroused in her such an upsurge of tenderness that she eased herself around the door, slipping down the steps and rested a hand on his shoulder, murmuring, 'Travis, what is it?'

He tensed at her touch, half raising his head. 'Go back to bed!'

She saw instantly what he had been doing. Or trying to do. The floor around his chair was littered with crumpled pieces of paper; the sheet left in the typewriter was blank. She pulled up a chair and sat down. 'You're trying to write,' she said prosaically. 'Travis, that's wonderful.'

He reared himself up on his elbows and glared at her as if he hated her. 'Don't nursemaid me, Paige, and don't feed me all the clichés about writer's block. I know them all, believe me. Just go back to bed and leave me alone.' He added belatedly, running his fingers through his hair, 'I'm sorry I woke you.'

'How long since you sat in front of a typewriter?'

'Too long, obviously.' His chair grated against the floor as he stood up. He walked over to the window; but he could not see out, for the lamplight only reflected his own image in the glass.

She was reminded instantly of their joined images shimmering on the surface of the lake, and of what had followed: perhaps the strongest tie that bound her to this complex, unhappy man, although by no means the only one. 'Have you any idea what you want to write?' she asked non-committally.

'If I did, I wouldn't talk about it,' he said rudely, thrusting his hands in his pockets. 'Laugh if you like, but when I wrote those two screenplays for the moguls in Hollywood I offended the gods. They're jealous and possessive and they won't be mocked. I forfeited my talents, Paige, I drove them away and they won't come back.'

When she went to stand beside him, the window threw back the outline of a slim figure in a peach-coloured gown. 'It's a lot easier to blame the gods than to take responsibility for yourself.'

'Don't lecture me! I can't write, Paige—that's what I'm trying to tell you.'

'You mustn't give up so easily!' she cried. 'You know you won't be content with your life in Teko Bay forever—chopping wood and catching grayling. There's so much more to you than that.'

He threw the words at her. 'Since when did you become such an expert?'

Gathering all her courage, she said quietly,' Perhaps since we lay together on the grass by the inlet, Travis. You learn a lot about a man when you make love with him, because it's the kind of intimacy that dissolves all the usual disguises.'

'Are you an expert on that as well?' he said unpleasantly.

'No.' her smile was full of self-derision. 'Far from it. When I was twenty I spent one weekend with a young man who for thirteen days was my fiancé, until his parents decided my antecdents were neither distinguished enough nor rich enough to grace the family tree. I don't think in San Francisco in the eighties you'd call that being an expert.'

As if the movment hurt him, Travis turned to face her and dropped his hands on her shoulders. 'I'm sorry, Paige—I shouldn't have said that. And I'm sorry about your fiancé, too. You must have been hurt.'

'Hurt and angry. Part of growing up, I guess. What I'm

trying to say, Travis, is that making love with Harold was nothing like making love with you. Somehow you reached the core of me, the part of myself that I've always kept inviolate, untouched by anyone. And because we were joined so intimately, I know you in a way that a thousand conversations like this could never reveal you. I know you have things to say, and I know you can and must say them.'

Her words seemed to hang in the air between them, as if each one were visible. Paige stepped back, freeing herself from his clasp, appalled by what she had so unwittingly revealed about herself in her urge to heal him. The poverty of her love-life. The shattering effect of his lovemaking. Biting her lip, she wished herself a thousand miles away, and heard the wail of the wind echo ironically in her ears.

Travis reached out and grasped her by the elbows, pulling her so close that she could see the individual stiches in the neckline of his T-shirt and feel the heavy pounding of his heart. 'Maybe I do have something to say. But that's not much good if I can't find the words to say it, is it? I can't write, Paige—*I can't find the words.*'

His voice broke. Paige took him in her arms, holding him with all her strength, and felt his body's trembling as if it were her own; his cheek was resting on her hair, his fingers digging into her back with a force of which she was sure he was unware. Her embrace was the only comfort she could offer, for she could not write for him. No one could.

She had no idea how long they remained locked together, although her spine was cramped and one foot asleep by the time Travis raised his head. He looked wrung out, deep lines engraved in his features. Then he kissed her on the forehead, a kiss without passion that she sensed was his way of thanking her for helping him through a dark night of the soul; and she was suffused with a quiet happiness that he had allowed her to help.

'What brought you here?' he said sombrely. 'In less than

two weeks, you've changed my whole world.'

'Brent brought me,' she said, knowing it was the only answer she could give him. 'He's the one who's changed your world, Travis. Not me. He's the one who'll stay here with you.'

'You won't stay.'

Although he had phrased it as a statement, she answered it as if it had been a question, and marvelled at the steadiness of her voice. 'No, Travis, I won't stay.

'One of these days you'll tell me why.'

She folded her arms around her body, abruptly aware of the scantiness of her attire, and told herself there was no reason to see his words as a threat. 'Speaking of Brent, he'll be awake with the birds tomorrow . . . so maybe we should get some sleep.'

'You're still running, Paige.'

'I'm being sensible, Travis, that's all. Goodnight.'

Had he tried to delay her, she would have been helpless to prevent him. But he did not try. As she climbed the stairs to her room, she knew he was watching her and felt his gaze burn through the fabric of her gown to her flesh, as if he had indeed laid his hands upon her.

CHAPTER SEVEN

THE NEXT day Travis looked very tired, his eyes deepset and shadowed, his movements without their usual unconscious grace. Paige's spirits were weighed down with a kind of despair, for it seemed that the more she tried to pull away from him, the more she was drawn into intimacy with him. Although the rain had stopped, the wind still tossed the branches of the great pines, and when she walked down the track she found the waters of Lake Tahini churned into untidy waves and driven spray. She could see the village today; it mocked her with its illusory closeness, for she knew without asking Travis that the lake was as impassable now as it had been yesterday.

She would take Brent to the Camerons and go and see Theo Herrick, she decided. That would at least have the merit of keeping her away from Travis.

An hour later Paige was tramping along the ridge trail beyond the Camerons. Brent was playing with Beth and Fiona, so she was quite alone, and content to be so. The leaves of the balsam poplars looked newly washed after the rain, a polished shiny green as they danced in the wind, and the clouds were as white as sheets blowing on a clothes-line. Her ankles brushed against some juniper shrubs, releasing their heavy, pungent scent into the air. Behind them, in a tangle of shrubs, tiny scarlet soapberries twinkled in the sporadic sunlight.

The trail climbed for nearly two miles, then gradually descended as the neck of land between the lake and the inlet narrowed. She crossed this land bridge and began another ascent. Felix had warned her to watch for a narrow path branching off to the right beside a pine that had been struck by lighting, for Theo's cabin could not be seen from the trail. That would be too public by far, thought Paige with a smile when the charred and twisted trunk of the pine finally came into sight. The pathway wound sharply downhill towards the inlet. She was not surprised when the four dogs erupted through the trees and surrounded her. She spoke to them quietly while they sniffed her legs and hands, wondering if Theo would be pleased to see her today, or if he would run for the woods.

'Mr Herrick!' she called out. 'I've come for a visit.' And she continued down the path. It ended in a clearing near the water's edge. For a moment Paige stood in silent appreciation, for the two brothers from England had known what they were doing when they had settled here.

The cabin was backed by a grove of poplars and evergreens that swayed in the wind, and on its far side was flanked by a creek that chuckled to itself as it tumbled to the inlet; plumed fern arched over its bed. A beach of pale sand lay in front of the cabin, which overlooked the heaving, sullen waters of the inlet and the gaunt, brooding mountains.'

Theo opened the door, poised like an animal for flight on the worn stone step. Paige said softly, 'This is the most beautiful place I've ever seen.'

He was wearing exactly the same clothes as yesterday, including the hat; she wondered if he wore it to bed. He did not speak. She said with a forwardness that rather horrified her, and with her most charming smile. 'I'm going to throw myself on your mercy and ask for a cup of tea—it's a long walk from Travis's.'

Short of rudeness, Theo was caught. 'You'd better come in,' he said.

The interior of the cabin was spotlessly clean and sparsely

furnished, dominated by a black pot-bellied stove on which a battered kettle simmered, and by one wall that was entirely lined with books. 'Travis has hardly any books,' Paige remarked.

'Travis should be writing them,' Theo said gruffly.

'That's what I've been telling him.'

'Hope he listens to you more than he does me.' Theo dumped a large scoop of tea-leaves into a Pyrex pot, added water and set it on the stove. 'Dogs didn't bother you today?'

'No.' She grimaced shamefacedly. 'Today I knew they weren't wolves.'

'One of them is.'

'Oh,' Paige said faintly, remembering how all four had sniffed her fingers. 'Which one?'

'The grey one with the yellow eyes. Raised him from a pup, his mother and father had been poisoned. No call to be afraid of wolves. They're better than people, the way I see it. Faithful to each other. Good parents. They fight sometimes, I know, but they never kill each other the way we do.'

It was Theo's longest speech. Paige said thoughtfully, 'Our fear of them goes back to childhood . . . look at the fairy-tales. *The Three Little Pigs. Red Riding Hood.* The wolf was always the villain.'

'Lot of nonsense.' He was cutting big slabs of home-made bread. He put them on the table and poured the tea, which had been boiling merrily on the stove.

Although the milk was canned and the sweetener molasses, a combination Paige would normally have shunned, Theo was offering her the best he had. Stirring her tea, she said, 'Nell told me your brother died recently,' and knew this was why she had come.

He was spreading butter on a piece of the bread; briefly the knife faltered. 'January,' he said.

'You must miss him very much.'

'He died in his sleep in his own bed, which is what he would have wanted,' Theo said stoically.

The tea was like no other beverage she had ever tasted, but the bread was delicious. 'My brother died two years ago,' Paige blurted.

Theo raised his head, so that she saw the strange yellow eyes. 'He was young, then.'

'Seventeen.'

'Well,' said Theo.

'So I understand a little of how you feel.'

'What was his name?'

'Martin. We called him Martie.' She chewed hard on the bread, feeling the familiar tightening of her throat.

'You're still angry about it, aren't you?'

She stared at him. No one had ever understood that before. 'I've never been able to cry,' she confessed. 'My mother wept and wept, and then died of a heart attack two months after Martie died. But I couldn't cry.'

He reached for the pot and topped up her cup. Higher than it had been before, she noticed with an inward wince. Then he asked, 'What happened to him?

'He got in with a bad crowd at high school, got hooked on drugs, dropped out of school and started stealing to support his addiction. He refused to come home . . . preferred living on the streets. There was a minor earthquake one morning, just a tremor. But it was enough to topple an old wall where he and his friends were camped. He was killed instantly.'

This was a litany Paige had repeated before. She braced herself for sympathy, horror, disbelief, and heard Theo say, 'If you can't cry, what *are* you doing?'

'I made a vow,' she said defiantly. 'I swore I'd do everything I could to keep kids like him off the streets. So I work for social services with delinquent boys. I'm going back as soon as the weather clears.'

'Does it help?'

'Of course! I'm saving boys from ending up like Martie.'

'Never figured anyone could save you except yourself.'

'I'm there to help them, Theo. Someone's got to.'

Theo did not look convinced. 'When are you going to look after yourself?'

'I can't stop working! That would be totally selfish.'

'I decided a long time ago that unless you're right with yourself, you might as well forget the rest of the world. You know what you should do? Find a rock down by the water, sit down, and cry your eyes out. Sorrow can't be locked up. I discovered that a long time ago, too.'

He would have been a striking man in his youth with those strange gold eyes, thought Paige, and wondered what sorrows had come his way.

'You think about it,' he said.

She did not want to think about it. Not once since her self-imposed vow had taken effect had she ever allowed herself to doubt it. The frustration and disappointment of the job itself, her growing fatigue, Barbara's lectures, even Travis's comments: none of them had caused her to question the validity of her task. She had to do it. She had no choice. Was she now to allow a half-crazy old man who had lived his life in seclusion to fill her with doubts? Her mouth set stubbornly, she reached for the milk.

Theo suddenly chuckled. 'My brother was a stubborn man. No mule I ever knew could get the better of him. You remind me of him. Same look about you.'

'Theo,' Paige said in exasperation, 'the world is full of people who won't put themselves out for others. You don't know what life is like in San Francisco; how can you criticise what I do?'

'Spit it out, Paige,' he said amiably. 'Tell me I'm a crotchety old bachelor who's been a hermit for years, and what do I know about real life?' As she flushed, for that was indeed what she had been thinking, he went on, tapping his gnarled finger on the table for emphasis, 'You'd be surprised how many people you come across in these mountains. Ordinary people. People with problems and sorrows and disappointments. People who just want someone to listen to them and tell them that they're real and that somehow it all means something . . . Do you know what I figured out a long time ago?'

Although she shook her head, he had not been waiting for her to answer. 'You help out wherever you happen to be.' Another emphatic rap on the table. 'You do what's right under your nose.'

'That seems too easy,' she said weakly.

'Tisn't always easy, no. But wherever you are, there are people who need you—you don't have to scurry around to find them, and you don't have to half kill yourself when you do find them. Defeats the purpose.' He reached for the butter. 'After all, you found me today, right?

'Are you saying I've helped you today?' she asked suspiciously.

'I've had the need to talk to someone about my brother, someone who'd understand.'

Unexpectedly her eyes filled with tears. 'I haven't even asked you his name.'

'Harvey. Eight years older, he was . . .'

'Did he look like you?' Paige asked.

As if her simple question had unloosed a floodgate, Theo began to talk. Fascinated, Paige listened as through the eyes of one old man and the history of the gold rush and the lake-boats and the prospectors unfolded. The two brothers had roamed these mountains together for years; and now one of them was gone.

She asked questions; she listened with the intentness of one who is genuinely interested; she drank more of the dreadful tea without noticing; until eventually Theo said, 'Well . . .' and Paige knew the story, for now, was over. He got up and put a couple of sticks of wood in the stove, and the crackle and spit of the fire broke the spell.

She said softly, 'Thank you for telling me all that, Theo—I'm complimented. But I'm going to have to go soon, because I have to pick up Brent and take him home. May I come again?'

He scratched his head and said ingenuously, 'Thought you were going back to the big city soon as the weather cleared?'

She had forgotten about San Francisco and the pressures of her job. 'I have to go back!' she said with a touch of desperation, and could not have said if she was trying to convince herself or Theo.

She stayed a few minutes longer, but the rapport was gone. As she waved goodbye to Theo from the path, buffeted by the dogs, she wondered if she would see him again. The dogs accompanied her to the top of the slope, then sat in a row, watching her as she walked away.

Everything that Theo had said was circling in Paige's brain, round and round, incapable of resolution. Sit on a rock and cry your eyes out, he had said. But it was not that simple, she thought, as she crossed the narrow bridge of land between the inlet and the lake, where rocks at the edge of the water abounded, any number of them smooth enough to sit on. She could not erase Martie from her life any more than she could erase the vow she had made.

Paige's father had died when Martie was only seven and Paige eleven, and their mother had not remarried. Was it the lack of a male role-model that had driven Martie to the gang of boys in high whose influence she had so deplored? Pleas, threats, reason, she tried them all and none had any effect; when she'd attempted to get professional help for Martie's drug problem he'd left home. Six months later he was dead.

Paige had failed him. Or so she believed. But she would

not fail again, and to that end she worked at her job ten and twelve hours a day, driving herself unmercifully and, in the occasional small victories, comforting herself against the loss of her brother. Now Theo was suggesting she change that pattern, as had Barbara before him.

She had reached the Camerons. She heaved a sigh, knowing she was not ready to make any changes, and went inside to get Brent. They walked home hand in hand, and as the little boy rambled on about the events of the day, she knew she should be telling him she was leaving soon. But I don't know when, a voice argued inside her. Maybe it won't be tomorrow. What's the point of upsetting him unnecessarily?

When she saw Travis, the first thing she said was, 'Is the wind dropping? Will I be able to get away tomorrow?'

Brent was chasing Minto through the trees. Travis gave her an unfriendly look. 'I don't know why you're in such an all-fired hurry to leave here.'

Perhaps, she thought edgily, because she wanted to return to certainty. She might have been exhausted in San Francisco, but at least she had known what she was doing. Here she was riven by doubts on all sides, assailed by emotions she had never felt before, confused by contradictory allegiances. She said with attempted indifference, 'I've told you often enough. What was the forecast, Travis?'

'The wind should die down overnight. So the lake might be calm enough by late tomorrow for you to leave. If, of course, I choose to take you.'

She raised her chin. 'If you won't, Felix will.'

'Clever little Paige,' he said mockingly, 'she's covered all the angles. The only one she's left out is a small boy's feelings.'

Could the man read her mind? Paige said fiercely, 'The sooner I leave here, the less of a blow it will be to Brent.'

'So you do admit it will be a blow?'

She had never thought of herself as a woman of violence;

it would, however, have given her a great deal of satisfaction to have wiped that sneer from Travis's face. She said in deliberate provocation, 'How many pages did you write, Travis?'

The sneer vanished. 'None.'

'Still blaming the gods?'

She saw his intention a fraction of a second too late. He seized her in his arms, bent his head and kissed her, a kiss that began in anger but swiftly became as provocative in its way as her words had been.

Brent said with evident interest, 'Felix kissed Nell today . . . Fiona says they do it a lot. Sometimes my mother used to kiss my uncles.'

Travis and Paige fell apart, Paige red-faced. Brent's brows were knit in unaccustomed thought. But then he brightened. 'Nell 'n' Felix are married. Fiona said so. You could get married. Then I'd have a mother as well as a father.'

Appalled by this five-year-old logic, Paige gabbled, 'Oh, no, Brent, we aren't going to get married. I have to go back to the city.'

With open belligerence, Brent said, 'Not today.'

'No, not today, it's too windy. Maybe tomorrow, though.'

'I want you to stay here,' he declared, as if that was the final word on the subject. 'When's supper?'

He looked like a miniature tyrant, his legs spread, his lips pouting. 'As soon as we get it,' Paige retorted spiritedly.

He gave her the endearing grin he had copied from Beth. 'OK,' he said.

How was she going to leave him? she wondered helplessly, feeling Travis's eyes on her and trying to look calm and competent, rather than beleaguered. Travis murmured, 'Now, if I were your fiancé, my mind would be on much more basic matters than your parentage and your lack of money.'

'I bet they would. Matters that would have nothing to do with getting married, though.'

'I'm not so sure about that. It could be that what we shared by the inlet is rarer than you think.'

'So rare that we shouldn't disillusion ourselves by doing it again,' she snapped.

'You haven't actually been asked.'

Theo's option of sitting by the lake and bawling her eyes out was beginning to seem more and more attractive, though not for the reason she had advocated. 'Supper,' Paige announced, and led Brent towards the cabin. But all though the meal and the long evening she was aware of Travis watching her. Aware with her body, she thought painfully. Wanting him. Yet knowing in her heart that to make love with him again would be the most dangerous course of action she could follow.

Predictably, she did not sleep well. At two in the morning, when she woke for what seemed like the hundredth time, she realised that the cabin was bathed in silence. The wind had dropped.

She would be able to leave Teko Bay today.

She lay still, dry-eyed in the darkness, listening to Brent's steady breathing and to the absolute silence from the other room, and wondered what she would do if Travis asked her to stay.

He wouldn't ask, though. He'd be glad to see her go. He had said himself that she had turned his life upside down . . .

The next time Paige woke, she was looking straight into a pair of violet eyes. 'You're a sleepyhead,' Brent accused.

Tomorrow morning she would wake up in a hotel room in Whitehorse. Reaching over, Paige enveloped Brent in a hug. He wriggled free indignantly. 'Let's get up.'

She would have liked to pull the duvet over her head and miraculously whisk herself to that hotel room without having to suffer through any of the events in between. 'What do you want for breakfast?' she said in resignation.

After breakfast Brent went outside to see the kittens. Paige began washing the dishes, so deep in thought that she gave a telltale start when Travis spoke behind her. 'The lake's calm—you could leave by mid-afternoon, Paige. If that's what you choose to do.'

His voice had been without expression. She turned around, wiping her hands on the towel, and said with the same lack of emphasis, 'Yes. That's what I'll do. Will you take me across?'

'I'll ask Felix. Under the circumstances, I think I should stay with Brent, don't you?'

'Stop dumping guilt on me, Travis!'

There was plenty of expression in his voice now. 'If the shoe fits, wear it. Have you said anything to him yet?'

'I didn't know I was leaving until two minutes ago.'

'Well, you'd better prepare him—I think he'll take it hard.'

She said curtly, 'I'd like you to look after him for an hour or so this morning so I can say goodbye to the Camerons. Then I'll speak to him.' Unable to meet his eyes, she took the dish-towel from the rack and started to dry a cup.

Travis grabbed both the towel and the cup, and flung them on the counter. 'You can at least look at me when you're talking to me! So even though you've got two more weeks off, you're determined to leave?'

'Of course,' she said coolly. 'I'll save the time for later. I do have my living to earn, Travis. Some of us can't afford to sit back and do nothing for five years.'

'You really can be a bitch when you put your mind to it, can't you? So what it comes down to is a matter of dollars and cents. Not a small boy's feelings.'

'Travis, had you accepted Brent from the start, I would have been gone two weeks ago, and Brent wouldn't have had the opportunity to grow so fond of me.' He could scarcely argue with the truth of that, she fumed.

His eyes gleamed. 'You know, I could follow Brent's suggestion and ask you to marry me. That way you'd stay.'

'Don't insult me,' she said shortly, fighting back a wave of bittersweet pain whose intensity shocked her. 'You don't even like me.'

As if she hadn't spoken he went on, 'Then you'd be in my bed legitmately.'

'Travis, stop!' she blazed. 'I'll tell Brent in my own good time, and a week after I'm gone he'll have forgotten me.' She turned back to the sink, scrubbing at a plate as if her life depended on it, her vision filmed with tears.

'Fine!' he said savagely. 'Go back to San Francisco and save all those others boys, and don't spare a thought for the one you've left behind in Teko Bay.'

'You're being horribly unfair,' Paige choked, her head bent, the tears now a blur between her and the soapsuds.

Her russet hair curled over the nape of her neck, where the skin was a smooth, pale gold. Travis said in a strange voice, 'Yes, I am, aren't I?'

The door burst open and Brent fell into the room. 'The kittens have got their eyes open! One of them's got blue eyes just like me, c'n I have that one for my very own? I'll call him Tom, like Tom Kitten, OK?'

Answer him, Travis, Paige prayed. Because I don't think I can even find my voice.

Travis cleared his throat. 'Sure, that's OK.'

From the corner of her eye Paige saw Brent jump up and down with excitement as he grabbed Travis's hand. 'Come on out with me now and see them, come along!'

Travis touched her on the shoulder; the contact shivered through her whole body so that she dropped a couple of knives into the sink with a great splash. 'I'll be back in a minute,' he said. 'We have to continue this conversation.'

As soon as they were out of the door, Paige dried her hands, found a scrap of paper and scrawled on it, 'Gone to Camerons',' and hurried out of the door herself, running up the slope as if all Theo's dogs were after her. Not until she was well out of sight of the old oak tree did she slow down, panting. The wilderness was getting to her, she thought wryly, for she was behaving like an animal herself, going on instinct rather than reason: instincts that were telling her to get away from Travis, with his touch like the shimmer of sunlight on her skin and his inexplicable anger; from Theo, who wanted her to save herself; from Brent, with his demands and his big violet eyes. Reason, of course, pronounced that she had two more weeks of holidays and the most logical place to spend them was here.

Nell obviously did not think she should leave, but chose not to argue with her, and gave her a handwoven scarf in subtle shades of blue as a goodbye present, while Felix agreed to take her across the lake after lunch and presented her with an exquisite hand-carved eagle. The two girls were bewildered by her departure. Paige walked back to the cabin, clutching her gifts. The colour of the scarf reminded her so strongly of Travis's eyes, and the eagle of their lovemaking, that the hotel in Whitehorse began to seem like a sanctuary. And she still had to tell Brent.

When Paige got back to the cabin, Brent and Travis were outdoors, measuring for an extension Travis was planning to build as a bedroom for the boy. She went inside to pack, then made some sandwiches for lunch. She had a hollow sensation in the pit of her stomach.

Then Travis disappeared into the tool shed. She called Brent in. He came quite happily, chattering away about the shelves he would have, and the built-in bed with drawers underneath, and shomehow this gave Paige the opening she needed. 'You do understand that Travis is your real father,' she began. Brent never called Travis by name.

Brent gazed at her warily, alerted by a change in her tone. 'Not like an uncle,' he agreed seriously.

'You'll always have a home with him, and he'll always love you.'

'And I can play with Beth 'n' Fiona.'

'That's right. You see, I have to go back to my home, Brent. I can't stay here any longer—that's why I'm glad you have your father and your friends.'

His lip stuck out. 'You're gonna stay here, too.'

'No, Brent. I'm leaving this afternoon.' There. She had said it.

'I don't want you to!'

Paige tried to put her arms around him, but he wriggled free. 'I have to. My home isn't here—it's a long way away, in San Francisco, remember?'

He was scowling ferociously. 'You can live here. With us.'

'I can't, Brent. But I promise I'll write to you.'

Brent was not old enough to marshal cogent arguments, nor was he old enough to tell her, as Pedro would have, what she could do with her letters. His lip began to quiver and his eyes filled with tears. Flinging himself at her, he wailed, 'Don't go, Paige! I don't want you to.'

He almost knocked her off balance. He was sobbing in earnest now, great whooping sobs of mingled rage and misery; she hugged him tightly, knowing she had not felt this powerless since the day Martie had died. Then Travis came in the door.

He said flatly, 'I'll take him. You'd better pack.'

But Brent refused to relinquish her, crying all the harder and clinging to her with the deceptive strength of a limpet to a rock, so that Paige had a mad vision of him being literally torn from her arms as she climbed into Felix's boat. She said helplessly, 'Travis, what will I do?'

She was kneeling on the floor, Brent's head buried in her breast. Travis hunkered down beside her, his blue eyes as guarded as she had ever seen them. 'You have two choices,' he said. 'You can leave right now. I'll look after him. He'll cry himself to sleep, as children do, and eventually he'll forget you.'

Paige dropped her cheek to the tousled brown curls. 'Number two?'

'Stay another two weeks. That'll give you the time to really explain why you have to go, get him used to the idea so it's not so traumatic . . .'

'Or just prolong the agony.'

He ignored her comment. 'I'll be honest with you, Paige. I'm not sure he's actually accepted me as his father. Two more weeks should build up a lot more trust.'

She had had the same doubts herself; it was the most convincing argument Travis could have used. 'I can't help him accept *you*,' she said stubbornly.

'You'll have to decide that, won't you?' He came closer, so close that she could see the taut seams in his jeans and count the dark hairs at the base of his throat. 'There could be a third choice, Paige.'

She glanced up with some of Brent's wariness. 'Oh?'

'We could take Brent's suggestion and get married.'

Clutching the boy's shuddering body, she said coldly, 'This is not the time for jokes, Travis.'

'I'm not joking.'

She discarded any number of scathing retorts. 'You only found out two weeks ago that you were a widower.'

'Stephanie has been dead to me for years.'

'After an experience like that, I wouldn't have thought you were in a hurry to remarry.'

His face was very serious. 'Do you know what I'd worry about, Paige? What if I do find I can write again? Writing isn't an ordinary nine-to-five job. What if the book took over and I neglected my second wife the way I did the first?'

'Not every woman would tear off and find herself a lover,'

Paige said with asperity. 'Some women do have resources of their own, you know . . . Oh, Brent, do hush!'

'You'd be just as likely to find yourself a job and put in so much overtime that *I'd* never see *you*,' he said, with such quizzical warmth that her heart skipped a beat.

'Travis, we can't get married to suit a five-year-old boy,' she said breathlessly. 'That's like the plot out of a Victorian novel.'

'Nursemaid marries lord of the manor?' he murmured. 'Some manor.'

She giggled, then said reprovingly, 'This is supposed to be a serious discussion. About my departure.'

'You look very sweet, Paige. I think he's been listening, he's not crying as loudly as he was.'

If it weren't for Brent, I'd be hauling that man off to bed, Paige thought clearly. But, if it weren't for Brent, I wouldn't be here at all. What am I to do? She turned her head to look out over the mountains, hating them for their stolidity, their indifference, even as she wished she could be like them. It was her decision. Hers alone.

Brent was still clutching her blouse, which was soaking wet where his face was pressed; he was blubbering her name like an incantation. 'How can I leave him like this?' she cried, and answered her own question. 'I can't. I'm a sentimental idiot, I'm every kind of a fool, and I'll regret this decision, I know I will—but I'll stay two more weeks.'

Travis sat back on his heels, and imperceptibly the line of his jaw relaxed. 'Good,' he said.

'Is that all you've got to say?' Paige demanded.

'That's all for now.'

His eyes were not guarded at all. She felt her body leap to life and said loudly, 'Brent, I'm not going today. Do you hear me? I'm going in two weeks instead.'

Brent raised his head. His eyes were puffy and his cheeks drenched with tears. 'Not today?' he snivelled. She shook her head. 'Not tomorrow?' Again Paige shook her head. 'OK,' he said, and gave one last hiccuping sob.

Paige said, not knowing whether to laugh or cry, 'Nell and Felix both gave me goodbye presents . . . who's going to tell them I'm not going?'

'You,' said Travis with an unholy gleam in his eye. 'It was your decision.'

She said, genuinely curious, 'What would you have done if I'd said yes to your proposal of marriage, Travis? Taken the first boat to Nelson's Landing?'

'I'm a man of my word,' he said piously. 'I'd have gone through with it.'

'I don't understand how Stephanie got bored with you,' Paige said in exasperation. 'You're a complete enigma to me.'

'Years ago my father gave me some advice. Keep 'em guessing, he said. That's the way to handle women.' Travis grinned at her. 'Works every time, right, Paige?'

'Oh, go chop some wood!'

'I've got a better idea. After lunch, let's go to the village, you and I and Brent. We can pick up some groceries and I can order the lumber I'll need for the bedroom. I might even treat you to dinner at The Cosy Corner.'

She felt light-headed from the release of tension. The decision, for better or for worse, was made. 'Best offer I've had all week,' Paige said, fluttering her lashes.

He could not possibly guess how peculiarly her heart was behaving . . . could he? You've had it, Paige Montgomery, she thought hopelessly. You're offered dinner in a two-bit restaurant in a village the size of a postage stamp, and you're as excited as if you've been invited to the best place in San Francisco. And, admit it, when he smiles at you like that, you're also delighted that you're staying another two weeks.

In a surge of recklessness that would have pleased Barbara, Paige decided to enjoy the next two weeks. She would pay for it in the end. But at the moment fourteen days seemed like a very long time.

CHAPTER EIGHT

WHEN Paige woke up the next morning, outwardly nothing had changed. She was in Travis's bed under the duvet, Brent snuggled into her side, while a robin was singing in one of the pine trees as it did every morning. But inwardly, she thought in wonder, she had woken to happiness.

She had rarely allowed herself to feel happy since Martie had died. She had made her vow, got on a treadmill, and had been running faster and faster ever since. Maybe happiness takes time, she thought, creasing her brows. Maybe you have to stop in your tracks and take a deep breath in order to smell, if not the roses, the pine trees. She lay still, conscious of Brent's weight and of Travis's quiet movements in the next room, and let the happiness warm her like the rays of the sun. It was fragile. It was undoubtedly fleeting. But it was real.

She, Travis and Brent had had a wonderful time in Nelson's Landing the day before. They had done nothing out of the ordinary, shopping for groceries, buying rubber boots and a toy for Brent at the little general store, eating a hearty if unimaginative meal at The Cosy Corner. Paige's strongest sensation was of being part of a family. After her father had died, her own family had disintegrated, her mother sinking into depression, Martie leading a life of his own, despite Paige's efforts to draw him into a threesome. Last night the three of them had felt like a family quite naturally, without strain. She had enough common sense to recognise this was dangerous, and enough of yesterday's recklessness not to care.

134

The cabin door closed and she heard Travis's voice outside, ordering the dogs to stay. Easing her arm free of Brent's body, she got up and padded into the living-room, looking out of the window just as Travis, who had a pack strapped to his back, disappeared behind the old oak tree. He must be going to Theo's with supplies, she thought, and wondered with slight unease why she had not told him she had met Theo.

He had left a note on the table to the effect that he would be back for supper, and would she mind looking after Brent? Rather to her surprise, Paige was not displeased to have a day to herself without the distraction of Travis's presence, although all day she was aware of looking forward to seeing him again.

For supper she made spaghetti, garlic bread and a salad out of vegetables from the garden; Brent was already at the table when the dogs barked to signal Travis's return. He came in the door, gave Paige what she secretly termed one of his enigmatic looks, and smiled at Brent. 'I can see I'm late . . . what have you been up to, Brent?'

Brent was not averse to describing his doings. Paige served the spaghetti and sat down, and as the meal proceeded was forced to admire Travis's dexterity in entertaining Brent while not making it overly obvious he was ignoring her. He must be annoyed she had not told him about meeting Theo. Too bad, she thought mutinously. She didn't have to account to Mr Travis Renshaw for every minute of her time.

Travis bathed Brent, put him to bed and read him a story. Paige cleaned up the dishes and went outside to give the salad scraps to Bentley the horse. She was standing by the paddock with Bentley nuzzling at her palm when Travis joined her. Going on the offensive, she said, 'I met Theo quite by chance, and as I assumed I would be gone by now, I didn't bother mentioning it to you.'

'Why didn't you tell me you had a brother who died?'

The westering sun, sinking towards the mountaintops, outlined her profile in gold. She shrugged. 'You never asked.'

He took her by the arm. 'I've told you about Stephanie, and about how I can't write. But you're like the proverbial clam—mouth clamped shut.'

'I told you about my engagement!'

'I don't think that short-lived engagement had nearly the impact on you that the death of your brother did.'

He was right. Paige bit her lip, hurt that Theo had betrayed her confidence. 'So did Theo tell you everything?'

'He wouldn't tell me a damn thing! Just happened to mention that it was too bad about your brother, and when I asked what brother, he came over all coy and said he'd figured I'd known about it or he wouldn't have said anything. Like hell!'

Like hell indeed, thought Paige. Theo did not trust her to save herself; Theo was trying to get Travis into the act. Scratching Bentley's ears with great concentration, she related the bare facts about Martie's death in a voice from which any emotion was erased. It did not take long.

'Now fill in the details,' Travis ordered.

'It was two years ago—there's no point. Anyway, I don't like talking about it.'

'He's the reason you panic every time San Francisco is mentioned,' Travis said inflexibly. 'He's behind that job of yours, I know he is. Give, Paige. Because we're staying here until you do.'

The gold flecks in her eyes were like tiny sparks. 'Confidences can't be forced,' she said.

'I thought you liked me well enough that you might choose to confide in me.'

'He's dead, Travis—dead and gone. He died two years ago because of a silly accident when he was high on drugs, and yes, he's the reason I do the best I can to keep young kids off the streets. Wouldn't you if you were in my shoes?'

'How old were you?'

'Twenty-one. He was seventeen.'

'Your parents must have been devastated.'

'My father's been dead for years, my mother had a fatal heart attack a couple of months afterwards. Travis, I really hate this inquisition!'

'Do you have any other brothers or sisters?'

'No.'

'Have you ever sat down since he died and cried until you thought you wouldn't have a single tear left?'

She turned on him accusingly. 'You did talk to Theo!'

'I did not! It stands out all over you, Paige—with the best of intentions you took on a job guaranteed to drive you into the ground, and you've never allowed your grief its natural course.'

Paige stared at the mountains. The setting sun was perched rather vulgarly on one of the peaks; the scene looked like a cheap postcard. 'You should be writing a book about me,' she said shrewishly. 'You seem to know a lot more about me than I know myself.'

'You know it—you just won't admit it.'

Which was unanswerable, thought Paige, because it was probably true. The sky was now a crude mixture of pink and orange, and Bentley had lost interest in her and wandered off. She wished Travis would do the same.

'Have you ever told anyone exactly how it happened and how you felt at the time?' Travis persisted.

'There was no one to tell. I'd only been home from university for a short while, Harold was long gone, and my mother was ill.' She dug into the fence with her fingernails. 'I didn't know Barbara very well then.'

'So you carried it all on your own.'

'Stop feeling sorry for me!'

He stilled her nail with his hand. Her wrist was as rigid as an iron bar, and when he tried to take her in his arms she stood stiffly, suffering the embrace without in any way surrendering to it. He gave a sigh of exasperation. 'Paige, can't you at least see me as a friend who, like Barbara, wants what's best for you?'

Staring fixedly at his shirt button, Paige said, 'I don't know how I see you, Travis.'

He gave another sigh. Then he answered with matching honesty, 'I'm not sure how I want to be seen . . . we're a fine pair, aren't we? I do know this much—when you first came here I didn't want you turning into a real person, which is, I suppose, why I didn't ask you any questions about yourself or your family.' His arms tightened around her. 'You're real enough to me now, Paige. And surely what we're here for on this earth is to share our joys and sorrows?'

To tell you I'm more than half in love with you? Paige pushed him away and said vaguely, 'Maybe some day I will. It's getting cold, Travis, let's go in.'

The sunset was approaching something like sobriety. Briefly she glanced over at Travis. He was leaning on the fence, one foot on the bottom rail, his face an inscrutable mask. But she was not deceived. He had offered her friendship and she had rejected his offer. Her reasoning was valid: she was terrified of discovering that she was deeply in love with him. But he would not understand that.

'You go ahead,' he said. 'I'm going to chop some wood.'

Her mouth twisted. 'As you're no doubt aware, California's noted for all its schools of therapy—from Primal Scream to Gestalt. Do you think there's one called Woodpile Therapy? Will you let me stack while you chop?'

He shook his head. 'You'd better go in.'

'I'm sorry, Travis,' she said helplessly. 'I know I hurt you.'

'It's not just that.' He pushed himself away from the fence

with barely controlled violence. 'Every now and then it hits
me like a ton of bricks just how much I want to make love to
you. Look at you now. Because your jeans shrank the other
day when you dried them in the sun, they sure don't leave
much to the imagination. The way your breasts push against
your shirt drives me crazy Your throat narrows to that little
hollow, and I can see the points of your collarbones and
almost feel the softness of your skin.' He raked his fingers
through his hair. 'It's all right, you don't have to run and
hide, I'm a grown man and I'm not going to do anything
about it—you've made it pretty plain you don't want to
make love again. But it sure would make life easier if you
took yourself somewhere out of range.'

Paige had flushed scarlet at the beginning of this speech.
Gaping at him, she babbled, 'I'm sorry, I didn't realise, I'll
stay in the cabin . . . oh, hell, what an awful mix-up this is!'

She discovered that she was wringing her hands. Feeling
absurdly self-conscious, and quite unable to think of
anything sensible to say, she turned away from him and ran
for the cabin. Once inside, she went straight to the big
window and looked out, her hands pressed to her hot cheeks.
Travis had lifted a huge chunk of wood on to the chopping
block and was swinging the axe with a concentrated energy
that spoke volumes.

So he thought she didn't want to make love. How wrong
he was! Yet wasn't the sensible course of action to allow him
to continue under that misapprehension, even if it did seem
to cast doubts on his ability as a lover? Two weeks was not
an eternity, however much she might wish it to be, and
Travis was not saying he was in love with her.

The blade bit into the wood, which sprang apart into two
cleanly split pieces that arched through the air. For a
moment Travis rested his weight on the shaft of the axe, his
head bent, his spine a vulnerable curve.

He might not be in love with her. He had, however,

offered her friendship. He was not a man to do that lightly—and she had thrown his offer in his face. I can't stand this, Paige thought clearly. I have to do something.

Her face brightened. Hurrying to the porch, she took a pair of Travis's jeans and one of his shirts from the hook, and tugged them on over her own clothes. After adding a pair of his old workboots, which she laced to the knee in an effort to keep them on, she crammed a battered stetson on her head, then looked down at herself. The cabin did not boast a full-length mirror; but she was willing to bet she did not look sexy.

Walking with difficulty, for the boots seemed to have a mind of their own, she navigated the cabin. Travis had put another log on the block and had the axe held high, ready to swing, when he caught sight of her. Slowly he lowered the axe.

'I've come to help,' she called.

He leaned the handle against the block and started towards her, his easy long-legged stride in contrast to her awkward shamble. 'The Abominable Woodsman?' he queried gently. 'Should I be fleeing in terror?'

'Woodsperson,' Paige corrected him.

'The sex is rather difficult to ascertain.'

'Exactly,' she said blandly.

'So I am to be discouraged from rape, ravage or rapine?'

Paige chuckled. 'I don't think you're that desperate.'

He reached over and tilted the stetson a little to one side, then stepped back and surveyed the result. 'You shouldn't be too sure of that,' he murmured.

She could feel herself beginning to blush again. 'You could chop and I'll stack,' she said severely.

Travis looked her up and down in a leisurely way. 'It's unlikely I'll be distracted by your figure—it seems to have disappeared,' he drawled. 'So I should be able to keep my mind on the job.'

She picked up the axe, gingerly running one finger along the edge of the blade. 'It might be advisable.'

He began to laugh. 'And what branch of therapy would you say you're representing, Paige Montgomery? The Escaped Lunatic School?'

She put down the axe, sat on the block and rested her chin on her hands. 'I guess I just wanted to make you laugh. We seem to fight an awful lot, don't we, Travis?'

'That's because we're both assertive, independent, and hellbent on getting our own way,' he agreed gravely. 'Now, if you'd only let me possess you on the sawdust pile, we wouldn't have to fight at all.'

'Sawdust makes me sneeze.'

He threw up his hands in mock complaint. 'Not a woman who's easily satisfied.'

The smile disappeared from Paige's lips. On the shore of the inlet he had satisfied her completely and felicitously, as if their bodies had been fashioned for each other; she had no reason to doubt that the sawdust pile would be any different.

As though he had read the fleeting expressions on her face, Travis said roughly, 'That ridiculous outfit doesn't make the slightest difference, Paige. Let's get to work.'

Tripping over her own feet, she stumbled away from the block as he grabbed the axe and made a vicious swipe at the log. Giving him a wide berth, Paige started carrying the newly split wood to the lean-to near the tool shed, where she stacked it methodically, one row in one direction, the next at right angles. The work was physical and real, and the results tangible in a way Paige's job in San Francisco almost never was; she got used to the vagaries of Travis's boots, and the confusion in her mind gradually subsided into peace. Travis was taking smooth, efficient strokes now, the logs falling apart as if under a charm. Like most activities, she was willing to bet it was not as easy as it looked.

As she loaded three birch logs into her arms, she said

impulsively, 'Travis, the problem with your writing isn't that you have nothing to say . . . it's finding the words, right?'

He gave her a cautious look. 'That's near enough. There's something about that first blank page—it's totally inhibiting.'

She sat down on one of the huge chunks waiting to be split. 'Why don't you start off writing about anything, anything at all? As a way of overcoming the blank page.' She warmed to her theory. 'I've been watching you split wood. You could describe how it feels to swing the axe through the air, the jar to your muscles when it digs into a knot, the way the chips fly, the hollow sound when the wood is rotten . . . that would fill a page, wouldn't it? Or describe the life Theo's led in these mountains, searching for gold for sixty years.' She cocked her head in the oversize hat and concluded naïvely, 'Maybe if you filled ten pages with nonsense, the eleventh page would be real.'

To her relief, he did not seem to resent her interference. 'There's a fancy name for that process—free fall. I suppose it might be worth a try. Anything's worth a try at this stage . . . You really care, don't you, Paige?'

She looked around her, not wanting to answer him directly. 'This kind of work is all very well. But it doesn't use your real talents. They're buried, Travis. Buried like the gold in the mountains.'

'Yeah . . .' Restlessly he banged the blunt end of the axe against the block, looking around him like an animal locked in a cage. 'Let's pack it in, Paige, it's nearly dark. I'll put the tools away.'

So Paige trudged up the hill alone, hauled off her extra clothes in the porch, and retreated to the bedroom to read. When Travis entered the cabin, she contented herself with calling goodnight, nor did he made any attempt at conversation. She was tired, so she turned off the lamp;

the light from the other room shone through the cracks around the door. An hour later she was still awake and was debating whether to pick up her book again when she heard, like miniature gunshots in the silence, the first tentative tapping of the typewriter keys. Her whole body tensed.

A series of taps. Silence. The keys clacked again. Another long pause. But gradually the tapping grew more confident and the pauses shorter, until finally it was as if a dam had burst and the words had come flooding out. Paige lay back, smiling in the dark, and eventually she was lulled by the rhythms of the typewriter keys into a deep sleep.

Brent woke her in the morning. 'He's asleep,' he whispered loudly. 'P'rhaps he's sick.'

Paige put her finger to her lips, inwardly wishing Brent could bring himself to call Travis something other than 'he'. 'Get dressed, and you can play outdoors for a while before breakfast.' She got up herself, slipping into her clothes, and tiptoed into the living-room with Brent. Travis was lying flat on his back on the couch, his chest bare, one arm flung over his head; he was breathing deeply and steadily. The typewriter was sitting on the table beside an untidy heap of papers. None of the sheets was blank.

Overcome with elation, she ushered Brent out of the porch door, where he was greeted by the two dogs, and went back inside. Because the cabin was never very warm in the mornings, she lifted the blanket over Travis's chest.

His eyes opened and smiled into hers; he was instantly awake. 'I did it!' he said exultantly. 'Fifteen pages of garbage, and three pages that just might be going somewhere. And it was because I knew you believed in me that I had the guts to stick it out.' He seized her round the waist and pulled her down on top of him, a position she found she liked very much. 'Paige, Paige, how am I going to thank you? If you hadn't nagged me like a harpy——'

'I did not!'

He nestled his face into her neck. 'Don't argue . . . we fight too much, remember? Mmm, you smell nice. Where's Brent?'

'Outside,' she said unwisely.

'Let's hope he stays there. Kiss me.'

Paige did not argue at all. She kissed him with passionate gratitude that he had found his voice again after so many years of silence; and then she forgot about the book, locking her arms around his neck, closing her eyes and surrendering to an elemental hunger more compelling than any she had ever known. His hands found her breasts, and he groaned deep in his throat. She fumbled to undo the buttons of her shirt, aching to feel her naked flesh against his hair-roughened chest.

It was Travis who called a halt. He tore his mouth from hers, his eyes the fathomless blue of the lake, and gasped, 'Paige, we can't—Brent might come in at any moment.'

He must have felt her trembling; she lowered her head, her brown eyes clouded, as if she was not quite sure where she was. He added, more gently, 'I've discovered one thing—you want to make love as badly as I do. Why did you lie to me?'

Paige pushed herself up, bracing her weight with her palms flat on his chest. 'I didn't really lie, Travis. It's as though I've been split in two . . . like the logs.' She hesitated, searching for words that would be truthful, without revealing how she felt about him. 'We talked about not having a casual affair, didn't we? We agreed it wouldn't be right for either of us. I know I can't have an affair lightly . . . and I know I'll be gone from here in less than two weeks. So the sensible part of me says stay away from you.' Her sudden smile was endearing. 'And then there's the rest of me.'

'Which is like a wildcat.' As she ducked her head in embarrassment, Travis added strongly, 'Don't ever be ashamed of showing me passion, Paige. It's the most real part of you, the part you've locked away for two years.'

'I don't know what's real any more,' she admitted in a low voice, staring unseeingly at the springing black hair on his torso. 'I came up here to do a straightforward errand for a friend, my life more or less under control, my priorities straight. Or so I thought. Then you and Brent and Theo and the mountains . . . you've confused me utterly. But mostly you.'

'I don't want to sound like a proponent of one of your therapy groups, but confusion can be a sign of growth, Paige.' He paused. 'Tell me something else—how long is it since you did something crazy, like dressing in those clothes last night?'

'Ages. Barbara says I've become very dull the last year or so.'

He tweaked her ear. 'I'm going to give you some advice. Take some time to think about all this—you owe it to yourself.'

She sighed. Then she levered herself free of him, doing up the top button on her shirt with fingers that seemed to find the task very complicated. 'I'd better get breakfast . . . are you going to write today?'

'We're not finished with this conversation, you know that, don't you?' Then he went on in a more normal voice, 'I'll write in the evenings, as long as that doesn't disturb you. The days will be for Brent.' He stood up, shaking off the blanket; as he stretched in front of the window, she watched in fascination, spellbound by the slide of muscle over bone and by the beauty of his long body. 'I want to mix the concrete for the foundation for his room today,' he added casually. 'He should like that—wonderfully messy stuff.'

How could Travis talk about concrete and his plans for the day when her body was burning and every nerve on edge? Paige thought crossly as she folded the blanket and punched the cushions into fluffiness again. 'I think *I'll* swim Lake Tahini,' she snapped.

'A rather drastic cure for sexual frustration, Paige, my love.'

'Don't call me that!' She thwacked the last cushion against the arm of the chair. 'Afterwards I might go for a five-mile run and chop a cord of wood.'

'You're making me feel wonderful, you realise that?'

'I'm glad one of us feels wonderful,' she retorted. 'And don't tell me I'm behaving childishly, I know I am.'

'A lot better for you than keeping your feelings locked up. More fun for me, too,' he added, winking at her.

She fired the cushion at him. It caught him full in the chest with a most satisfying thump. As he threw it back, she ducked, then lunged for it. But he had had the same idea; they collided at the end of the couch. 'Oof!' said Paige, whose breath had been knocked from her lungs.

Travis threw back his head and laughed as Paige had never heard him laugh before, a full-throated belly laugh that was irresistibly contagious. 'If you could have seen the expression on your face,' he gasped, and lifted her right off the floor in a bear-hug. 'Oh, Paige, what am I going to do with you?'

She would have liked to have known the answer to that question. But then Brent pushed open the door and said, 'What's so funny?' and she never did get a reply.

Later in the day, when Travis and Brent were absorbed in the making of concrete, Paige walked to Theo's. He greeted her by asking, 'Did you find that rock yet? Now that you're staying.'

She scowled into the strange amber eyes. 'I'm only staying two weeks. No, I didn't find the rock. Travis hasn't found it for me, either.'

Theo gave a dry hack that seemed to pass for a laugh.

'Travis doesn't know what to think as far as you're concerned. Haven't seen him as edgy in a coon's age. Not that I can advise him, an old bachelor like me.'

'I don't think you're the slightest bit backward in giving advice,' Paige declared. 'However, I didn't come for advice today, I came for another piece of your delicious raisin bread.'

'Well,' said Theo. But her compliment had pleased him, she could tell, and she managed to persuade him to make coffee rather than tea, in which the molasses might not taste so overpowering. When he had everything served, he said conspiratorially, 'I've decided to show you something. Because you stayed. You wait here.'

Paige munched the thickly textured bread as he disappeared outside. When he came back in, he was carrying a small wooden box; undoing the brass clasps, he took out a gold ring. 'My brother made this from the very first strike we had, back in 1925. Over by Chilkoot Pass, it was. He gave it to me then and I've kept it ever since.' He dropped the ring into her palm. 'Pure gold,' he said, and in his voice was the longing and the awe that had driven him and those like him to spend their lives in these lonely mountains.'

The ring was heavy. Paige slipped it on her finger, admiring the surprisingly delicate design of flowers and interwoven leaves that had been carved into the gold. 'It's beautiful, Theo,' she said.

'Back then I figured I'd find a woman to give it to. But somehow I never did.' He shrugged philosophically. 'Too late now.'

She took it off her finger and put it back in the box in the cotton wool in which it had been wrapped, feeling his loneliness as poignantly as if it were her own. 'Now that your brother's gone, it must be particularly precious,' she murmured, and wondered why he had chosen to show it to her.

She was not to find out. He grunted something and took the box outside with him to restore it to its hiding place, and entertained her for the rest of the afternoon with stories of various husky teams he had owned. Paige walked home deep in thought, unable to avoid the implications of a gold ring that had stayed hidden in a box for sixty years. Theo had not found anyone to give the ring to. Theo had bypassed love. Theo was alone now, without children or grandchildren to call his own.

When she got back to the cabin, Travis and Brent were both outside, and neither of them noticed her approach. Travis had built wooden forms for the foundation of the new bedroom, and was pouring the cement from an old wheelbarrow, his muscles straining in the long line of his back, which was beaded with sweat and smeared with dust. Brent was slapping at a mound of cement with a paintscraper, his dirty face one big grin of contentment.

Paige retreated as quietly as she had arrived. They did not need her, she thought painfully. They were perfectly happy without her.

Not knowing what else to do, she busied herself in the kitchen, baking cookies, then making a very elaborate meatloaf with an assortment of vegetables and a salad. She was washing lettuce at the sink when Travis came in; he had sluiced the worst of the dirt off in the rain barrel. He grinned at her. 'I could get used to this—coming in after a hard day's work to find supper ready.'

'We women have our uses,' Paige said, far more sharply than was warranted.

He took her by the elbow. 'I was just thanking you, Paige. No need to call me a chauvinist.'

He smelled of the sun, and mortar, and sweat, and his tanned skin was only inches from her face. She pulled free. 'Where's Brent?'

'He's coming . . . what's wrong with you?'

The door burst open. 'Hey, Dad, guess what! Minto walked on the cement and you can see his paws in it.'

Travis swung his head round. In a peculiar voice he said, 'What did you call me?'

Brent made a swipe at his nose, which was running. 'Dad,' he said, obviously puzzled. 'That's OK, isn't it? You're my dad.'

'Oh, yes,' Travis answered dazedly, 'yes, that's OK.' He suddenly bent and swooped the boy up into his arms, hugging him tightly to his bare chest. 'I thought you'd never call me that,' he said in a muffled voice. 'Brent, I love you. You're my son, and I love you. I'll always be here for as long as you need me, do you understand?'

Brent tried to squirm free. 'Don't you want to see what Minto did?'

His face dazzled with happiness, Travis said, 'Sure, Sure, we'll go right now.' The boy still in his arms, he left the room.

Paige closed her eyes and leaned against the wall. *I love you*, Travis had said. But he had said it to Brent. Not to her. She was glad Brent had accepted Travis as his father. Truly glad. But oh, how she wished Travis would say those words to her.

Her hands were pressed to her face and her throat ached with unshed tears. But she couldn't cry now, not when Brent and Travis would be coming back any minute and expecting her to serve the meal and make rational conversation. I've never felt less rational in my life, she thought. I love Travis. That's why I've been feeling so torn and confused. Because I love hom and I know I have to leave.

The porch door banged and she heard Brent's treble accents. Paige straightened, taking a sharp breath and trying to compose her features. The last thing she wanted to do was impose her own unruly emotions on them. She had to face the facts. They had each other now, and Travis had his writing; they would need her less and less. It had all worked out the way Travis had hoped when he had asked her to stay for two more weeks. Now, for her pride's sake, if for no other reason, she must try and fade into the background for the days that remained.

CHAPTER NINE

WHEN she looked back on the next few days, Paige realised very little effort was required on her part to fade into the background, because Brent and Travis were absorbed in each other to the exclusion of herself. She did not think it was intentional, nor did she think they meant to be unkind. They were simply making up for lost time. Travis for five years had not known he had a son; she watched his outpouring of love on the boy and recognised it to be both natural and healing. And, even though she was sure Brent's use of the word 'Dad' had been instinctive rather than planned, she saw a new sense of security in him. Brent knew he had a home with Travis for as long as he needed it.

In her heart of hearts, Paige could not quarrel with any of this; she would have given a great deal to have been able to provide Pedro, for instance, with the same sense of security. However, she was left the prey to a loneliness more acute than any she had ever known.

She tried not to succumb to it. She visited the Camerons and Theo and read the books that she borrowed from them; she forced herself back to her field guides and spent hours roaming the woods; she gardened and cooked. But she slept poorly, for the tapping of the typewriter keys were now one more thing that distanced her from Travis, and when she did sleep she was haunted by dreams in which she was lost among the mountains and the tall pines, searching for something which she would never find.

One morning, when the dreams had been particularly bad, Paige did not get up until Travis and Brent had left the cabin. She made a cup of coffee and sat by the window to drink it, looking out at the brilliant sunshine with lacklustre eyes. If she had any initiative, she would leave here. But that would involve explanations for which she did not have either the energy or the mental ingenuity; it was easier to stay. She leaned her head back against the chair and shut her eyes.

'Paige, are you ill?'

White-fanged wolves had been leaping at her through rings made of gold . . . Paige sat up straight and mumbled, 'No! Of course not. I was just asleep.'

Travis was appraising her clinically, his eyes narrowed against the light. 'You look awful,' he said. 'As tired as when you arrived. What's wrong?'

'Nothing! I'm fine,' she said, mentally crossing her fingers against the lie and adding pointedly, 'Shouldn't you be with Brent?'

'He's mixing the feed for the chickens . . . it's not him I'm worried about.' With the air of one who has made a decision, Travis went to the radio and called the Camerons. Nell answered. 'Will you do me a favour, Nell? Would you keep Brent for the day? I want to take Paige to Raven's Head. Over.'

'Delighted! If you're late home, I'll put him to bed here. Bring him any time you're ready.'

Travis cut the connection and came back to the window. 'I'll take him over there now, Paige. If you want to pack a few sandwiches we could leave as soon as I get back.'

'You have yet to ask me if I want to go!'

Swiftly he knelt at her feet, his hands clasped in front of him, his blue eyes laughing at her through the thick fringe of his lashes. 'Dearest Paige, will you embark with me in my freighter canoe, if not to Valhalla, at least to the mountain on Laird's Inlet, where I shall show you an abandoned mine shaft, a porcupine or two and no doubt some mosquitoes?'

Dearest Paige . . . She frowned down her nose at him.

'Give me one good reason why I should. and leave out the porcupine.'

'The view is fabulous? The air is the cleanest in the country? I can see you're not impressed.' He sat back on his heels, and for a moment the laughter died from his face. 'How about this? I'd very much like to spend the day in your company, Paige. I've neglected you lately.'

She did not bother denying this. 'We could take Brent with us.'

'He couldn't climb the mountain, it's too steep.'

'You're not trying to keep me from him, are you, because you know I'm leaving?' She had not realised she had been harbouring this suspicion until she had voiced it.

'I've been enjoying being a father, Paige. That's all.'

She flushed uncomfortably. 'I guess I shouldn't have said that.'

'Better to speak it than think it. Although it doesn't say much for your opinion of me.' He stood up impatiently. 'I'm going to take him to Nell's, and you can decide in the meantime if you want to come with me or not.'

She knew she would go with him, for it might be her only chance to spend a day alone with him. She had to leave in five days; San Francisco had never seemed so remote.

So, when Travis arrived back, Paige had neat packets of sandwiches and cookies ready on the table, and the canteen was filled with water. He looked at the food with a crooked smile. 'Enough for two?'

The table was between them, not entirely by accident. She and Travis were alone in the cabin, a rare occurrence that for Paige was fraught with mingled threat and promise. She wondered if he was as aware of this as she. She wondered what she would do if he were to take her by the hand and lead her up the stairs to the bedroom.

She said in a voice brittle with tension, 'Where's the boat?'

'Down at the dock.' He flung a haversack on the table.

'We'll put the food in this.'

But as she picked up the sandwiches he reached for the buckles, and their hands touched, his fingers curving around her wrist. Paige flinched as though she had been stung. Her heart began to beat in sick, heavy strokes.

He dropped her wrist, rubbed his hand down the side of his jeans, and said flatly, 'I'll get the life-jackets.' Without meeting her eyes, he left the room.

Paige stuffed the food in the haversack and went outside to join him. Anything to put distance between her and the bed, she thought with a desperate kind of humour, forgetting that the only time she and Travis had made love they had not needed a bed. Travis had already started along the track, walking as though pursued by demons. She ran after him.

The canoe was moored at the dock. After Travis had started the motor, they set off, hugging the shoreline until they came to the mouth of the river that flowed between the inlet and the lake. He turned the bow of the canoe into the current and headed upstream.

The sun danced on the turquoise water, the waves banging against the cedar ribs of the canoe, sending up sheets of spray that drenched Paige's hands. She yelled back at Travis, 'I'm glad we don't have to paddle up this!' and saw him gesture towards the sky.

One of the bald eagles had launched itself from a grove of spruce, and was circling higher and higher into the clear blue sky. In a flash of exultation Paige thought, This might be the last day I'll spend alone with Travis. I'm not going to be cautious and rational and safe. I'm going to live it to the full, with whatever it brings. And I'll remember it for the rest of my life.

They left the swift-flowing currents of the river for the calm of the inlet, and chugged along the shore, past the Camerons. Paige determinedly looked the other way when they approached the beach where she and Travis had lain together;

some minutes later she waved at Theo and the four dogs beside his cabin. Then the cabin disappeared from sight, leaving her and her companion alone in a world of tree-clad hills and harsh, bare mountains under the blue dome of the sky.

After Travis had cut across a wide cove, he edged into the shore again where the water was shallow and almost warm to the touch. He drove the canoe into some clumps of grass at the base of a grove of poplars, and Paige climbed out. The ground was soggy; a cloud of mosquitoes rose to meet her. She swatted at them futilely. 'We could stay in the canoe and drive around and around,' she suggested.

Travis laughed. 'Once we start climbing, we'll leave them behind.'

'Climbing?' She looked up. Through the green lace of the poplar leaves she could see steep slopes of tumbled boulders with a smattering of trees, and then gaunt outcrops of bare rock. 'How far?' she said darkly.

'Beyond the scree. No mosquitoes up there, Paige.'

'Are you an honourable man? To be trusted?'

'Plus there's a view.'

'I'd better be able to see all the way to Whitehorse,' she threatened, and slapped at a mosquito. Her fingers came away streaked with blood. Her blood.

'Come here,' Travis said. 'I'll put some dope on you before they carry you away.'

From his pocket he had taken a small plastic bottle, the contents of which smelled strongly of tar. Paige said indignantly, 'You're not putting that on me!'

'That or bleed to death. These aren't polite Californian mosquitoes.'

'You're enjoying this, Travis Renshaw.'

He shook out a few drops of the liquid on to his fingers and advanced on her. She held her ground, her face lifted, knowing as he began rubbing the repellent around her hairline that he was far more dangerous than a million mosquitoes. She wrinkled her nose. 'That ought to repel more than the bugs,' she remarked.

His hands were now smoothing her neck. 'You could be immersed in the stuff and I'd still want you,' he answered levelly, then passed her the bottle. 'Do the same for me, would you?'

He bent his head. Paige wiped the liquid on the nape of his neck, up into his hair, and over his forehead, and by some miracle neither spilled the bottle nor threw herself at the man. She passed the bottle back. He put the cap on. Then they both spoke at once.

'I don't——'

'How can——'

Travis said roughly, 'We came to climb the mountain, and that's what we're damn well going to do!'

'Yes, Travis,' Paige said meekly.

'You drive me crazy, you know that?'

'It's entirely mutual.'

'Oh, for heaven's sake!' He turned his back and began tramping along a faint trail between the poplars.

Paige had suffered so much herself the last few days that she was not displeased to see him suffer too. She buttoned her shirt to the very top, tied a scarf over her head and set off after him. But they had only gone a few yards when Travis stopped to point out a pair of redstarts flitting through the branches, and then the next excitement was the porcupine he had promised her, a fat, slothful one wedged in the fork of a birch tree. As they topped a little rise they saw the V-shaped wake of a beaver in the cove below, and the untidy heap of its lodge at the mouth of a creek. When the beaver dived, the ripples made concentric circles on the water.

Paige said spontaneously, 'When I first came here I was terrified of the woods—they seemed empty, silent, utterly different from the city. I've discovered since then that they're every bit as busy as the city, and just as interconnected and interesting.'

Travis gave her an unreadable look. 'Stephanie hated the outdoors,' he said, and set off through the trees again.

Half an hour later, still climbing steadily, they had left the poplars behind and were traversing grassy slopes scented with juniper and sage. The patches of grass became more sparse; Paige had to watch her footing rather than the scenery. She was gasping for breath by the time she reached what Travis called the scree, steep slopes consisting solely of treacherous, sharp-edged rocks where twice she started miniature avalanches. The clatter of rock on rock was incredibly loud.

'Not much further,' Travis said.

They crossed a second scree, then kept climbing on the diagonal, crunching the oval leaves of kinnikinnick and mountain cranberry underfoot. Travis was breathing normally. Paige pushed on, trying not to puff and pant too obviously, glad to see that the gaunt outcrop of rock that was beaked like a raven's head was getting closer. Travis took her hand to help her clamber over the last big boulders. Then he said, 'This is one of the old mine claims from early in the century—the shaft is down here.'

The shaft, surrounded by huge rocks and braced with hand-hewn logs, was a black hole that disappeared into the earth, depthless, bottomless. Paige pulled back, white-faced. Martie had died under a heap of rock. 'I hate it,' she muttered. 'I wouldn't go down there for anything.'

'Claustrophobia?' She nodded, for it seemed simpler than explaining. Travis added, 'Theo's found gold down there. He swears there's more to be found.'

'Theo can have it. Can we go somewhere else?'

'Sure. I promised you a view, didn't I?'

A few minutes later, when they had rounded the outcrop, Travis stopped on a small patch of grass and sat down. Paige looked around her.

Slightly above them the granite boulders of the mine shaft cut into the sky. But in front of her lay the inlet, backed by its jagged peaks whose outline was so familiar to her, and to her left lay the long, dark strip of land, hunched like the back of a bear, that stretched between the inlet and Lake Tahini. The village was invisible. But she could see the turquoise ribbon of the lake, the faraway mountains capped with clouds, and the white streak that was the glacier at the headwaters of the lake.

She said quietly, 'We could be the last people on earth,' and sat down with her chin on her hands to drink her fill.

Time passed. When Paige eventually turned around, Travis was asleep, his head resting on the haversack, his long body relaxed. He had been working late into the night all that week, persevering steadily with his writing, despite a number of setbacks, so she was not surprised he was tired. What took her by surprise was the surge of love she felt, a mixture of passion and tenderness that overwhelmed her in its intensity. What strange twist of fate had led her to this remote wilderness, there to discover her power to love?

He slept on, oblivious to her. On a more earthly plane Paige also discovered she was hungry and that Travis's cheek was lying on their lunch. To distract herself, she wandered further away from the outcrop, stooping to examine the juniper berries, finding an ant hill and nearby some bear droppings, reassuringly weathered. A small clump of poplars were growing into the mountainside below her; there might be birds there, she thought, and started inching her way down the loose gravel towards it.

Twenty feet above it her feet skidded out from under her and she landed heavily on her bottom in a shower of pebbles. Her momentum carried her downwards swiftly and gracelessly. She yelped in pain as her hip glanced off a rock. Trying in vain to brake herself, she bumped into the nearest poplar and tumbled head over heels into the grass.

For a moment Paige lay still, gathering both her wits and her breath. Then she cautiously moved her limbs one by one. She was just concluding that they all seemed to be in working order when she heard the sharp rattle of stones above her head. A rockslide, she thought in panic, and cowered into the grass covering her head.

'Paige! Are you hurt?'

Urgent hands were probing her body; and the voice was Travis's. 'I'm fine,' she gulped. 'I thought you were an avalanche.'

'Are you sure you're not hurt?'

Knowing exactly what she was going to do, Paige opened her eyes and rolled over, so that the hand that had been testing her ribcage covered her breast. She said softly, 'Travis, come here,' and lifted her arms, knowing that this was what she wanted more than anything else in the world.

She could see the desperate hunger in his face, and then the hesitation, the pulling back. 'Are you sure——' he began.

She touched his lips with one finger. 'Make love to me . . . please.'

His words were an uncanny echo of her own. 'There's nothing I want more in the world,' he said.

The first time they had made love it was as if they had been under a spell, all their movements slow and graceful and somehow preordained. But this time was full of impatience and humour and moments that were intensely real. Travis had a knot in his bootlace; as he wrestled with it, swearing lamentably, Paige was nibbling at his ear and reaching round him to unbutton his shirt. 'You taste of fly dope,' she complained.

'Don't expect me to kiss *your* neck, either.' With a grunt of satisfaction, he hurled the boot across the clearing. Then he suddenly turned on her, pinning her wrists to the ground and lowering his weight on her. 'Got you,' he said.

Her eyes were brimming with laughter and desire. 'I don't have fly dope on the rest of me,' she murmured.

Their clothes were discarded with awkward haste. Stones dug into Paige's back. An ant crawled across Travis's collarbone. The leaves dappled their bodies with sun and shadow. And through it all they made love with joyous abandon and a sweet intensity, as if they were indeed the last people on the earth and had only each other; and when Paige cried out in repletion it was like the call of a wild bird.

She lay in his arms and whispered, 'You won't leave me this time?'

'No, I won't leave you.' He hesitated, and for a moment she was sure he was going to say something else. But then, so fleetingly she could have imagined it, a look of the bitterest frustration scored his face and he looked away.

'Travis——' she said in alarm.

'Hush . . . lie still.'

Paige searched his features, seeing nothing now but a contentment that matched her own. Reassured, she gave a tiny sigh, draping one arm across his ribs and feeling his thighs hold her close. 'What would we do if a bear came along?'

'Tell him not to be a voyeur.'

'I'd love to go to sleep. But there's a root under my hip and my left toe has either disturbed an ant hill or it's lying directly in their migration route.'

'Ants don't migrate.'

In a flurry of breasts and limbs, she sat up. 'They bite, though!'

Travis pulled her to her feet. 'It's because you taste so good,' he said lazily.

Remembering in quite startling detail some of the things they had just done, Paige blushed. His arms were around her, their naked bodies touching from shoulder to knee in a way she secretly adored, and in a flash of insight she knew she would never forget this moment, or the man holding her so intimately in the shadow of the trees. Wordlessly she lifted her face to be kissed.

Travis kissed her so slowly and so tenderly that she was filled with happiness. In silence, they picked up their scattered clothing and dressed, then climbed back to the outcrop and ate lunch. Afterwards, hand in hand, they began the descent of the mountain.

CHAPTER TEN

PAIGE was left to her own devices the day after the mountain climb, because Travis was working on the foundation for Brent's bedroom. She did not regret what had happened on the side of the mountain, even though overnight she had been seized by the premonition that it would never happen again. Yesterday she had been too caught up in the glory of his lovemaking to miss the words he had left unsaid; today that omission was all she could think of. For Travis had not said he loved her.

Nor was he doing anything to prevent or delay her departure at the weekend. While she had kept her bargain and had spoken to Brent on several occasions, having established that she was not leaving that day or the next Brent paid her no attention. She shied away from picturing the actual moment when she would leave; her imagination could not deal with it.

She busied herself in all the usual ways. Mid-afternoon she squeezed some orange juice and put it on a tray with a few cookies for Travis and Brent. An offering of love, she thought drily, knowing Brent would accept it as his due and Travis would be grateful but nothing more. Balancing the tray carefully over the uneven ground, she walked to the back of the cabin.

Travis was measuring for the studs, his brow furrowed. Paige said with a sprightliness she hated, but that seemed to be the only way she could deal with him, 'I've brought you something to drink. How's it going?'

'Thanks,' he said, giving her one of the boyish grins that

always pierced her to the heart. 'Nothing like a bit of carpentry to take your mind off a problematical novel.'

As usual, he was naked to the waist; the muscles rippled across his shoulders as he reached for the glass. Her glance flicked away from him. 'I haven't liked to ask you about your work.'

He sat down on a heap of lumber. 'I don't want to talk about the book itself—I never do. But you don't know how good it feels to be writing again, Paige. I feel whole. I'm doing what I'm meant to do. Sounds pompous, doesn't it? But it happens to be true. I'm so aware of how much I owe you—I needed someone to force me into it. To believe in me.'

She seemed doomed to receive gratitude from him, when what she wanted was love. 'You're welcome,' Paige said lightly. 'Where's Brent?'

Travis looked around. 'He was here a minute ago.'

'I'll go and find him.'

She was a coward, she scolded herself as she went towards the chicken house and the tool shed. But how could she cope with discussions about a novel, problematical or otherwise, when she was racked by memories of yesterday's intimacy? He could have been talking to Nell or Felix a moment ago, rather than to the woman who the day before had held his shuddering body at the moment of climax.

Brent was not in either building. Paige checked the barn, then called his name. 'Brent—cookies and juice!'

His reply came from the vicinity of the old stone wall. 'I'm stuck, Paige. Come 'n' help.'

She threaded her way through the alders, trying not to snag her hair. Then, through the thick curtain of leaves, she heard the scrape and thud of falling rocks, so peculiarly reminiscent of the day before that for a moment she wondered if she was dreaming; until, following on it, Brent gave a yell of mingled outrage and pain.

She began to run, crashing through the bushes, twigs lashing her face and her bare arms. She could hear him crying now, loud howls that precluded serious injury but that were still alarming. She burst into the open, where the stone wall ran from the woods to the river.

Brent was lying under a heap of rocks; his forehead was streaked with blood. For a moment that was out of time Paige was transposed to a street in San Francisco, where an old cement wall had collapsed on top of a young man whose face had also been streaked with blood. Martie. His eyes had been closed and he had been lying ominously still, and the onlookers had moved back to give her room, dozens of pairs of eyes glued avariciously to her face . . .

Brent's heels were drumming on the ground and he was shoving at the rock on his chest, sobbing furiously. Fighting for control, Paige began lifting the stones off him, her voice wavering in her ears. 'It's all right, Brent. Lie still.'

Then Travis was beside her, elbowing her out of the way, tossing the last of the rocks as if they weighed nothing. His hands very gentle, he searched the boy's body for injury, so that again Paige had that sickening sense of *déjà vu*, as though time itself could not be depended on. 'Nothing's broken,' Travis muttered. 'I'll carry him to the house, Paige.'

He lifted his son into his arms. Brent was still crying, more from shock than from pain. Paige trailed after them, feeling as if she was trapped in a nightmare from which there was no escape. In the house she helped Travis like a robot, fetching water and clean clothes and the first-aid kit. The blood on Brent's face was from a superficial cut on his forehead, and apart from a few scrapes and bruises he was otherwise unhurt. Travis put him to bed, staying with him, the soothing rhythms of his voice drifting out into the kitchen. Paige cleaned up the mess. Then she slipped outside.

She was shaking so hard, she could barely stand. The sighing pine trees and the snow-capped mountains had no reality, for she was standing on a dusty street watching the ambulancemen load her brother's body into an ambulance. They were not hurrying; there was no need.

Blindly she looked around. The barn . . . she could hide in the barn. She stumbled across the grass and pulled the door open, and the scented darkness welcomed and enclosed her. Flinging herself down on the hay, she buried her face in her arms, trying to blank out the inexorable parade of images. But she had repressed them for too long. They crowded against her vision, overpowering her, until helplessly she began to cry. Then the crying itself overwhelmed her, the sobs tearing at her throat and racking her frame.

She did not hear Travis come into the barn, and only dimly was she aware of strong arms encircling her, and of the solid warmth of a man's chest, against which she was beating her fists and howling out a pain that was inconsolable. She had no words. Only a grief that had been penned up for months; grief black as the mine shaft on the side of the mountain.

In the end, sheer exhaustion quietened Paige, the physical inability to weep any more. Collapsed in Travis's arms, she gradually became aware of herself again as a person, an entity who could encompass her grief rather than be encompassed by it. Martie, she thought. Oh, Martie.

Travis's chest was wet where her cheek had been lying, and through her palm she could feel the steady beating of his heart. His said quietly, 'That was a lifetime of tears, Paige.'

Her voice seemed to come from another woman. 'My brother Martie got hooked on drugs when he was sixteen. He moved out of the house and lived on the streets for months with a whole group of his friends. They had a campsite on a deserted building lot where some warehouses had been partly demolished. Nothing I could do or say would persuade him to come home. One day there was a slight earthquake, just a tremor really, at ten o'clock in the morning, and I got a phone call at work from one of his friends telling me to go to the warehouse right away. An old cement wall had fallen on him—he had blood on his face, just like Brent. I got there at the same time as the ambulance; it only took them a minute to say he was dead.' An involuntary sigh tore at her throat. 'Not that I needed to be told. It was obvious.'

'You didn't cry.'

'I couldn't. There were people watching, and when I went to the hospital I had to sign all kinds of papers; I hadn't realised death was so complicated. And then the police came and I had to answer their questions. And after that I had to go home.'

'To your mother?'

'Telling her was the worst part of all. She sat as still as a statue for five minutes. Then this tirade of words poured out. She blamed me, you see. Me and my father. My father for dying and leaving her alone to raise her children, me for not being a good sister, for going to university instead of looking after Martie, for driving him out of the house, for not trying hard enough to get him home . . . it was awful. It was as if she'd hated me for years and I'd never known.'

Travis said wryly, 'So to compensate for grief and guilt you drove yourself into the ground for two years, trying to save all the other Marties in San Francisco . . . for someone who must have studied psychology, you weren't very smart, Paige.'

Emotion coloured her voice. 'That's easy for you to say. I owed it to Martie, Travis.'

'He may not have had his act together, Paige, but surely he wasn't so selfish that he would have wanted you to have a nervous breakdown trying to save every other kid in the city.'

'I was not going to have a nervous breakdown!'

'All right, maybe that's an exaggeration. But you were so tired when you got here, all you could do was sleep. And admit it—you haven't stopped fretting about your job the whole time you've been here.'

She pushed against his chest, struggling to free herself. 'It's a good job. It's worth doing!'

He was getting angry himself. 'Of course it is, that's not the point. But you can't use any job as a cover-up. As a way of avoiding the truth about yourself. That's not fair to the boys you're trying to help, or to yourself.'

In different words, Travis was saying what Theo had said. Paige was silent, her head bowed. Travis added, 'I'd swear on a stack of Bibles you've never cried for Martie the way you cried today. That should tell you something.'

He was right. 'It was because of Brent,' she said defensively.

It was his turn to sigh. 'Whom I've left alone in the cabin because I knew there was something wrong . . . Face the facts, Paige. You can't carry your brother for the rest of your life. Let the dead bury the dead.' He levered himself up from the hay, the trace of a smile on his face. 'I don't think I can better that as an exit line. Think about what I've said, won't you?'

She watched his tall frame move out of the door, where it was momentarily silhouetted in the light. Then he was gone, and she was left with her thoughts, and her ghosts.

Travis ignored Paige for the rest of the day, as though he had said what he wanted to say and had nothing further to add. Her storm of weeping had left her with a dull headache. She went to bed early, was asleep before he started to write, and woke up the next morning feeling thoroughly out of sorts. At nine o'clock, when she was making scrambled eggs for breakfast, Travis's number came over the radio-phone. The call was for Paige from Barbara.

'I've been wrestling with my conscience for the last five minutes,' Barbara announced. 'I didn't want to call you, but I was afraid you'd have my hide if I didn't. Pedro has run away, Paige. He left some time yesterday afternoon and he hasn't come back.' Hurriedly she added, 'Over.'

Paige clutched the microphone. She was not supposed to have favourites in her job, but Pedro's intelligence and

charm had been hard to resist, and somehow he had become
the symbol of her struglgle. Pedro. Her dingy little office. The
jazz drifting in her apartment window. All the noise and
colour and confusion of the city. She said, out of a deep well of
certainty, 'I'll come home, Barbara. I can leave here today
and go stand-by in Whitehorse. I'll call you when I arrive.
Over.'

'That was what I was afraid of,' Barbara wailed. 'A few
more days isn't going to make any difference, Paige. At least
wait until your vacation's over. Darn my stupid conscience!
Over.'

'I'm glad you called,' Paige answered crisply. 'I'll see you
tomorrow at the latest. Goodbye, Barbara. Over and out.'
She spoke briefly to the operator, then put down the
microphone.

Travis and Brent were both staring at her, identical
expressions of hostility on their faces. They had, of course,
heard every word she and Barbara had said.

Heartily glad of Brent's presence, Paige said with the same
crispness, 'I have to go back to San Francisco. Will you take
me across the lake, Travis?'

'We both will,' he said, his voice resonant with suppressed
rage. 'So we can wave as you disappear over the hill and we'll
know you've gone. You'd better hurry—there's a bus at
eleven. Lucky for you, isn't it?'

'Travis——'

'You didn't even take a second to decide, did you, Paige?
One tweak of the string from this Pedro and you're gone. My
feelings. Brent's feelings. Theo's feelings. They count for
nothing.'

'I was leaving at the weekend anyway,' she retorted.

'But that wasn't soon enough.' He suddenly banged his fist
on the table, so hard that the mugs jumped. Paige and Brent
jumped, too. 'I'm glad you're leaving today,' he went on
furiously. 'The sooner, the better. Brent and I will get on

with our own lives, and you can go back to your self-imposed martyrdom.' He thrust his fists in his pockets. 'Go and pack, Paige, so we can get the hell out of here.'

She realised she was opening and shutting her mouth like a stranded fish. She turned around and headed for the bedroom. Behind her, Brent said in a small voice, 'Where's Paige going, Dad?'

When Travis answered, it could have been a different man speaking; she stopped dead in her tracks. 'Paige has to go back to the city, Brent. It's where she belongs. We'll take her across the lake in the boat so she can catch the bus. It will be hard, and I know you'll miss her a lot, but we've both always known she'd leave sooner or later . . . it's OK for you to cry, but you mustn't try to make her change her mind like you did last time.'

Paige did not dare turn around. Feeling as rotten as perhaps Travis intended, she climbed the stairs and began to pack. This was the third time she'd prepared to leave Teko Bay, she thought wretchedly. Third time lucky. She was quite sure nothing would stop her departure today.

The motor on the canoe started on the first try and the lake was dead calm. Paige sat in the bow of the canoe, and Travis and Brent in the stern; she would have liked Brent at her side, but had not dared suggest it. Travis unloaded her gear at the dock. Then the three of them walked past the moored seaplanes towards The Cosy Corner, which also functioned as the bus depot.

The bus was parked near the petrol pumps. The driver was inside the restaurant, drinking a cup of coffee and carrying on a heavy-handed flirtation with the waitress. He stopped long enough to sell Paige a ticket and check his watch. 'Leaving in fifteen minutes . . . you can get on any time you like.'

Fifteen minutes seemed like an eternity, and the smell of french fries was making her feel sick. She said desperately, 'You don't have to wait, Travis.'

'We're not going straight home,' he said coldly. 'I have to see if the lumber I ordered has arrived, and then Brent and I will have something to eat.'

Brent and I. Feeling as though she was being split in two, Paige said clearly, 'I'm going to the Ladies. Excuse me, please.'

The Ladies was primitive but very clean. Paige stared at herself in the cracked mirror over the sink, and wondered how she was ever going to get through the next few minutes.

She managed to waste five of them by combing her hair, powdering her nose, putting on lipstick, and simply staring into space. Then another woman came in, giving her a peculiar look; Paige went back into the restaurant.

Brent was standing next to his father, his shoulders with a forlorn droop. Impulsively Paige knelt down beside him. Ignoring the dozen or so other occupants of The Cosy Corner, she said, 'Brent, I know you don't understand why I have to go—I'm not sure I understand myself. But I want you to know something. Your father will give you a good home and he'll always love you. You're very lucky . . . he's a wonderful man.'

She hugged him hard, kissed him somewhere in the vicinity of the nose, and stood up. 'I'm going to get on the bus now,' she said, her voice sounding too loud because of all the emotions churning in her breast. 'Thank you for everything, Travis,' she added idiotically; then she thought of some of the things that 'everything' entailed, and felt her cheeks grow hot. 'Take care of yourself,' she went on in the same loud voice. 'Goodbye.'

This isn't happening, she thought frantically. I can't be standing in a crowded restaurant saying goodbye to Travis. It's not possible. It's all wrong.

He said nothing at all. Putting his arms around her, he bent his head and kissed her thoroughly on the lips, a long, explicit kiss that he plainly had no intentions of rushing.

Someone behind them gave a piercing wolf-whistle. Paige surfaced long enough to kick him surreptitiously on the shins. He deepened the kiss, taking his time, and then finally released her. 'Goodbye, Paige,' he said.

His eyes were pools of burning blue. She closed her mouth, swallowed, grabbed her bag and fled from the restaurant. The door of the bus stood open; managing not to trip up the stairs, she found a seat near the rear and sat down.

The air was stifling. However, when Paige wrenched the window open all she could see was Brent, who was standing at the window-pane of the restaurant with his nose squashed against the glass. Then, to her infinite relief, the driver came out of the door, talking earnestly to the old man she had met the day she and Brent had arrived in Nelson's Landing; he was still chewing tobacco, she noticed, and she would swear he was wearing the same shirt. She studied him assiduously, her nerves at the screaming point.

The conversation ended. The bus driver climbed aboard and made a great ceremony of collecting the tickets he had just sold. He took his seat, revved up the engine so that the whole bus shook, and they lurched away from The Cosy Corner.

Brent was waving. Travis was standing behind him, immovable. Paige waved back. Then as the bus pulled out on the road, she clenched her hands in her lap and felt two tears splash on to them.

As if the gods in their wisdom wanted Paige back in the city, her journey went like clockwork and she was in her apartment by midnight. She fell into a dead sleep, and woke in the morning to the blare of foghorns from the harbour, the whine of the air conditioner, and the horrible sensation of not knowing where she was. She staggered out of bed and went to the window, noticing en route that all her plants had, not surprisingly, died.

All she could see was buildings. Tall and short, wood and

stucco, modern and Victorian. A sea of buildings. A forest of buildings. A wilderness of buildings. Oh, no . . .

She took a deep breath, willing herself to calmness. She would grow used to this again, just as she had grown used to waking to the sighing of the pines, the songs of the robins, and the small sounds of Travis moving around in the next room. Travis . . .

Clutching the window-frame with all her strength to keep herself upright, Paige stared unseeingly over the buildings. Travis was the crux of the matter. Not Brent, for all that she loved him; not Pedro, despite her concern; not her job. Travis was the one she could not live without.

She felt a million miles away from him, so that it scarcely seemed possible he existed in the same world. Perhaps he had vanished, she thought wildly. Perhaps she had dreamed him.

Perhaps she would never see him again.

She leaned her forehead against the window as pain gripped her like the squeezing of a vice. She had to see him again. She could not bear it otherwise. He had become as necessary to her as the air she breathed.

The telephone rang. The sound jangled along her nerves. Instinctively she knew that the person at the other end of the line would not be Travis; she could not make it be so. She picked up the receiver and said, 'Hello.'

'Darling, we don't have to say over and out and all that James Bond sort of stuff, what a relief. How are you? You don't sound quite all there—did I wake you up?'

'Hi, Barbara.' Paige took a deep, steadying breath. 'Culture shock, I guess . . . I travelled a long way yesterday. Is there any news of Pedro?'

'That's why I called. He came back yesterday afternoon all on his own, apparently he didn't get in any trouble, although you should check with the office, I suppose . . . I got in touch with your friend, Mr Renshaw, hoping you hadn't left, but I was too late. He didn't sound too happy with you, I must say.'

Just to hear Travis's name mentioned filled Paige with that same agonising pain. 'I had to come back,' she said shortly. 'I'll go down to the office as soon as I'm dressed. Could we meet for dinner, Barb?'

They agreed on a time and place, and Barbara rang off. Paige showered and dressed with grim concentration, then took a bus to the office. She had forgotten how shabby parts of the city were; rubbish was piled on the pavements, and the air was stale and gritty. The office windows needed cleaning, while the pane of glass that had been broken by a vandal had still not been repaired. The stairs creaked.

'Morning, Paige,' said the receptionist, her fingers busily typing the whole time she talked. 'Have a good holiday? We weren't expecting you yet—so Anna's still in your office. She may be taken on permanently, Mrs Solvero says. Go right along.'

Paige walked down the corridor. It seemed as though a hundred years had passed since she had last trodden the worn green carpet, and she felt like an interloper as she tapped on the door of her own office. An abrupt voice called, 'Come in.'

Paige had met her replacement before she left. Anna Hines was older than she, with a no-nonsense air rather at odds with the kind grey eyes. 'You've come about Pedro,' Anna said immediately. 'He shouldn't have left without telling us, of course. But he went to see his mother, to see if there was any chance of making a home with her. I could have told him there wasn't—but he had to find out for himself. I foresee him settling much better in his foster home now.'

So Paige's early departure had been for nothing; there had been no crisis. 'Has he stolen anything lately?'

'Not for two weeks.'

'That's a record,' Paige said. 'I don't understand.'

Anna smiled deprecatingly. 'This might sound ridiculous, but I've started him playing squash. Do you know the game? Extremely fast, requires a lot of stamina and a good eye.

It can be a great outlet for energy and aggression. Of which Pedro, under all that charm, has his fair share. He's taken to it like a duck to water—I teach it, you see, as well as play. I think he could very rapidly become a competition level player.'

Paige curved her fingers around the arms of the chair. Although in her university years she had been a competent basketball player and a more than competent volleyball player, she had allowed any outside activities to slide after Martie's death. It would have been better for Pedro if her personality had been more well-rounded, she thought humbly. Anna in one month had accomplished more with him than she, Paige, had done in six months.

She said quietly, 'I think that's wonderful. I hope you will be staying, Anna . . . we need some new blood here.'

'The grant went through two days ago,' Anna said briskly. 'So I'm safe for a year, anyway.'

After they had talked of other clients for a few minutes, Paige made a duty call on Mrs Solvero, her boss. Then she left the building. Standing on the pavement, feeling oddly at a loss, she wondered what she should do next. Pedro had a part-time job to save money for his squash membership, so there was no point in trying to track him down. She did not want to go back to the apartment.

She walked aimlessly along the crowded pavements until she came to an intersection where the out-of-town buses passed. She boarded an eastbound one, sat for several blocks and then got off. The cemetery where Martie was buried was across the street.

The roses were in bloom, and there were beds of massed petunias and geraniums. Paige wandered between the rows of headstones until she came to the simple slab of granite that bore Martie's name and the dates of his all-too-short life. Standing in the damp grass, she gazed downwards.

'I've come to say goodbye,' she whispered. 'Seems like a

funny thing to do after all this time, Martie. But I kept your death at bay with all those other boys, didn't I? I hid from myself and I never really lét you go.'

That was why she had come today. To tell him she loved him, and to say goodbye.

She stayed for perhaps an hour. Then, her face very peaceful, she left the cemetery and went back to the apartment. She washed her clothes, went to the bank and made some phone calls, and at six o'clock met Barbara in a salad bar three blocks away. Barbara hugged her, then held her at arm's length. 'You look different,' she said.

'Yes.' Paige smiled. 'I've finally figured out why I've been running for the last two years. I won't have to run any more.'

Barbara was frowning. 'I'm delighted to hear that, of course—but there's more to it than that.' Her brow cleared. 'I know—you're in love!'

Paige did not bother denying it. 'I'm going back, Barb. I have to.'

'Because of Travis Renshaw?' Paige nodded. 'Even on that dreadful telephone thing, he has the sexiest voice,' said Barbara. 'I don't know if he's in love with you or not, but he sure as heck was angry with you.'

'I don't know if he's in love with me, either. I guess that's why I'm going back, to find out.'

'This calls for a drink.' Barbara ordered two Pina Coladas and said, 'So my call didn't ruin your life?'

What if Travis never wanted to see her again? If he could not forgive her for leaving? Paige closed her mind against these dreadful possibilities and said slowly, 'Although I knew I had to come back yesterday, I didn't understand why. I do understand now.' Briefly she described what she had done that day. 'So you see, I had to go to the office and see that I wasn't indispensable. And I had to say goodbye to Martie.'

'Unfinished business,' Barbara said wisely.

'Exactly! Now I'm free to return to Teko Bay . . . Did

Travis really sound angry, Barb?'

'Furious,' Barbara said cheerfully. 'He must be in love with you, or why else would he care whether you leave or not?'

'I'm not sure it's that simple . . . What will I do if he's even angrier when I go back?'

Barbara studied her fingernails. 'Take him to bed.'

'We've already done that.' Paige's face was suddenly lit with radiance. 'It was wonderful . . . if he doesn't want me, I'll have to enter a nunnery. Because I can't imagine making love to anyone else.'

'You have got it badly, haven't you? Tell me more about this male paragon, Paige.'

Paige's narrative lasted until they were sipping coffee after their meal. She finished by asking despairingly, 'If he is in love with me, why didn't he ask me to stay? I know he asked me to marry him—but he wasn't serious.'

'Testing the water, maybe.' Barbara put her head to one side. 'All sorts of reasons. He had a bad experience in his first marriage. He had a classic case of writer's block—so he must have felt cut off from his real self. You come waltzing in with a son he didn't know existed. You and he do nothing but fight—and occasionally make love—for the best part of a month. And then you take off, the message being that your job is more important than him or Brent. Give him a break.'

'I suppose so.' Paige was poking at the last of her dessert with her fork. 'Barb, if he doesn't want me, I don't know what I'll do.' The eyes she raised were wide with terror.

'Of course he'll want you,' Barbara said stoutly. 'Look what a difference you've made in his life already.' She added with low cunning, 'But what would you do about your job, Paige?'

'Quit it,' Paige replied with a breathless laugh. 'I could find lots to do up there. Nell told me they have a terrible time finding social workers or teachers so far north.'

'Then marry the man.'

'Oh, sure. I'll knock on his door and say I was just passing by and would he by any chance care to marry me—I can imagine what he'd say.'

'He might say yes. Or he might ask you first. Don't be such a defeatist.' Barbara studied the bill. 'Whatever happens, you'd better get on that radio-telephone fast and let me know.'

'You and the rest of the Yukon,' said Paige, pulling a face. She raised her coffee-cup. 'To my success.'

They solemnly clinked their cups together. Some of Barbara's optimism had rubbed off on Paige; it lasted until she was in bed in her apartment, alone with the dead plants and the whine of the air conditioner. Then terror struck her again. Travis would not want her. Travis had let her leave without trying to stop her. Travis did not love her.

CHAPTER ELEVEN

TWO days later, at seven o'clock in the evening, Paige was walking along the ridge towards Theo's.

This had not been her original plan. Her original plan had been to arrive at Travis's unexpectedly and thereby shock him into an instant proposal. But Travis, she was told at The Cosy Corner, was in Whitehorse with Brent, and might not be back until the next day. When she had recovered from her dismay, she had crossed the lake with Dick and walked to the Camerons, where she had found a note on the front door to the effect that they had gone berry picking and would not be home until dark.

Theo, she had thought. Theo would be home, frying up some of the dried caribou meat on which he seemed to subsist, and boiling tea with molasses. She was hungry. She was also, she admitted to herself, slightly desperate for the sound of another human voice. She had travelled hundreds of miles the last two days, and no one was here to even say hello.

She swung along the path, certain Theo would be pleased to see her. She must tell him about Martie. Only another mile to go.

Paige heard Theo's dogs before she saw them. They were whining quite horribly, and then broke into a chorus of barking as they burst through the trees to meet her. There were only three of them. The yellow-eyed wolf was not with them.

Two of them nudged her hands, tugging at her and whimpering deep in their throats, while the others leaped and pranced in front of her like an animal that had been released from a cage. Paige said out loud, 'What's wrong, you guys? Where's Theo?' and started down the path to his cabin.

For a moment she thought they were going to stop her, for the black dog was banging against her legs, almost knocking her down, and the smallest one was worrying at her ankles. But then they parted ranks to let her through. 'Theo!' she called. 'It's Paige—I've come for a visit.'

There was no smoke coming from Theo's chimney, nor did he open the door to meet her. Teko Bay was jinxed, Paige thought, trying to quell a sharp pang of fear.

She hurried across the grass and pushed open the door, not at all surprised to find that the cabin was empty. Empty, but giving every indication that the owner expected to be home at any minute. There was a kettle sitting on the wood stove, whose round black sides were still warm; Theo had left a loaf of bread out on the table and a chunk of meat on the cutting board.

The largest of the three dogs had nudged her hand again and was pulling her towards the door. 'OK,' she said, 'I get the message. Something's wrong. But you'll just have to wait a couple of minutes.'

Moving as fast as she could, she packed some of the bread and a canteen of water in Theo's old canvas haversack, as well as a first-aid kit that looked as if it had come over from England in the nineteen twenties. She could not find a flashlight. At the last minute she left a brief scrawl on a sheet of foolscap to the effect that she felt something was wrong and she had gone looking for Theo. Then she was outside.

The three dogs turned left at the trail, lunging ahead of Paige, tails wagging; had they been able to speak, they could not have said more clearly that they were glad she had finally paid attention to them.

She had walked this section of the trail with Theo on one of their birdwatching expeditions, and knew it led eventually to the cove where she and Travis had landed the canoe the day they had climbed the mountain. Surely Theo had not gone that far? She had no desire to find herself on the slopes of the mountain with darkness approaching. She walked faster, trying to subdue the knot of anxiety in her breast. Theo had roamed these woods for sixty years . . . what could possibly have happened to him? Heart attack, she thought with a tightening of the knot. A broken leg. One thing was certain—he would not be lost. She might be. But not Theo.

She had passed the farthest point where she and Theo had ventured, and now she was on new territory. The trail was climbing steadily, the trees changing to lodgepole pine and gnarled poplars that let in more light than the spruce wood she had left. The dogs were silent now, full of purpose, occasionally glancing over their shoulders to see that she was following. When she emerged from the trees to a clearing, she saw that she was already above the cove.

Stopping for a minute to catch her breath, she realised with a sinking heart that she had not been very clever. She had left a note at Travis's to tell him she was back, and one at Theo's—but not one at Nell's. If Travis did not come home tonight, no one would think of looking for her. The Camerons had no way of knowing that she was within a thousand miles of here.

The smallest of the huskies nudged her forward. Steadfastly Paige began climbing the mountain.

Half an hour later her destination was becoming more and more obvious, for she and the dogs were now above the treeline, traversing the scree slopes that led towards the outcrop of rock called Raven's Head. The mine shaft, she thought with a chill up her spine. Travis had said that Theo still believed there was gold to be found down the old mine shaft. When she remembered the black, depthless pit, her spirit quailed.

The dogs were going more slowly, picking their way across the tumbled rocks with a care she did her best to imitate. She did risk a glance over the inlet, whose sheen of orange and gold, like a length of fabulous Oriental silk, was indescribably beautiful. But sunset meant darkness, and darkness was the harbinger of terror.

Her foot skidded down the side of a rock so that she banged her knee. Grimly Paige forced her attention back to the scree.

The gaunt boulders of the outcrop were full of shadows. As she stopped again to try and lessen the pounding of her heart and the whistling of air through her lungs, the lead dog gave a sharp bark. From the vicinity of the shaft came a joyous whine of welcome. She heaved herself over the last slab of granite, and saw the wolf and the black dog touch noses. Then the wolf sat on its haunches, lifted its nose to the sky and howled.

Every hair on Paige's neck stood up on end. Theo must be dead, she thought frantically, and breathed an equally frantic prayer that this not be so. The wolf howled again. The sound seemed to echo across the inlet and the darkening sky, where the first star glimmered over her head, and she found she was clutching the rock for support, the smallest dog pressed against her ankles.

Then, into the pulsating silence, Paige heard a voice. 'Help!' it said feebly. 'Anyone there?'

When she tried to speak, all she could produce was a faint croak like that of a sick cow. She cleared her throat and said foolishly, 'Theo! You're alive. I thought you were dead.' She pushed herself away from the rock, her knees weak, and stumbled towards the shaft.

The opening was black, a black unlike any she had ever seen before, impenetrable, dead, like the entrance to Hades. Paige crouched down and called, 'Theo, where are you?'

His reply came from deep in the pit. 'I fell,' it quavered. 'Figure I've sprained my ankle—can't put any weight on it. What in tarnation are you doing here, Paige?'

The blackness was not as absolute now. 'How can I get down?' she yelled, and the cowardly part of her hoped he would tell her not to do any such thing.

'Steps in the rock. Eight of them,' said the disembodied voice.

She peered downwards, discerning a ledge carved into the rock face, a very small and uneven ledge. All we need is another sprained ankle, she thought, and shouted, 'I haven't any light.'

'I've got a flashlight—been saving the battery.' And she saw a thin wash of light illuminate the tunnel.

She had no further excuse. Paige took a deep breath, stooped down facing the rock, and lowered one leg. Her foot found the ledge. She put all her weight on it and cautiously lowered the second one. Six steps later her questing foot touched on gravel.

When she had both feet firmly planted on the ground, she looked up. Silhouetted against the sky were the four dogs, a semicircle of flopping ears and black noses. Much comforted, she said, 'You stay—I'll be back in a minute.' Then she turned around, knowing she must trace the beam of light to its source.

The roof of the tunnel was so low and the walls so narrow that it took every ounce of Paige's courage to leave the shaft with its view of sky and strike out underground. She felt as though the whole side of the mountain was pressing down on her, squeezing her, waiting to crush her with its weight. She inched along, the dirt scuffing under her sneakers, trying not to touch the wet patches on the side walls as the tunnel led deeper into the earth.

But the light was growing stronger, and when she called out to Theo he sounded reassuringly close. Then the tunnel branched. The light was coming from the left fork, which soon deteriorated into a rock fall. Paige did not want to think about rock falls. Choosing her path carefully, she rounded a bend and saw Theo and the light simultaneously. His back was against the wall; he was surrounded by boulders large and small; he was grinning.

She grinned back. 'I wouldn't do this for everybody,' she said.

There was enough space for her to kneel beside him. Swinging the haversack from her back, she undid the buckles, noticing proudly that her hands were steady, and produced the canteen. 'It's only water—I didn't want to take the time to make tea.'

Theo drank long and deep, then eagerly chomped on a hunk of bread. Paige sat back on her heels. It would probably be dark outside now anyway, she thought philosophically, so she was in no hurry.

Wiping his mouth, Theo said, 'I knew the dogs would bring help. But I thought it would be Felix—not you. Where's Travis?'

She explained that Travis was in Whitehorse and the Camerons berry picking. But she was not to be let off that easily. 'Travis told me you'd left for good. Didn't sound best pleased. You come back here to marry him?'

She said rapidly, 'I came back because I couldn't stay away, but I don't think Travis wants to marry me. How's your ankle?'

'The gold ring's yours if he does,' Theo said craftily.

'Blackmail.'

He gave her another wide grin before looking down at his right boot, whose laces he had loosened. 'Devilish sore. And no one to blame but myself.'

Paige got to her feet. 'Theo, I know my limitations—there's no way I can get you over these rocks and up the steps, I'll have to go back to the Camerons and fetch

Felix. Will you be all right?'

'Take the flashlight,' he said, holding it out to her.

'I can't leave you alone in the dark!'

'How're you planning to find your way down that mountain without a light? Only a sliver of a moon right now. Git! The quicker you go, the quicker you'll be back.'

She bent and kissed him on the forehead. 'I'll go as fast as I can.'

'Not so fast that you break a leg,' Theo said gruffly. Then, as she climbed over the nearest rock, he added, 'Glad you came back to Teko Bay, Paige—we missed you, the dogs and me.'

She answered with a catch in her throat. 'Someone has to keep you out of trouble. 'Bye, Theo.'

The feeble beam of light trained on the ground, Paige picked her way to the fork in the tunnel. The floor was very uneven. To steady herself she braced her knuckles against the wall. But the rock was wet and slimy; when she jerked her hand away with an exclamation of disgust the flashlight flew from her grasp and smashed on the ground. She was plunged into darkness.

'You OK?' Theo quavered.

'I dropped the flashlight. But I'm almost at the shaft,' she called back over her shoulder with false confidence.

The darkness was absolute, thick, cold and damp. Paige could hear the tattoo of her heartbeat, but she could not see her own two feet. She took a step, then another, and knew the ground could drop off in front of her and she would have no warning. She forced herself to touch the walls, to take another two steps, then two more. The silence was as thick as the darkness, the scrape of her sneakers on the rock exaggeratedly loud.

The floor of the tunnel seemed to be sloping downwards, and in a flash of panic she wondered if she could have taken the wrong turn at the fork. Sweat broke out on her palms.

She could be going deeper and deeper into the heart of the mountain with every step she took.

Don't be a hysterical fool, Paige, she berated herself. You're heading towards the shaft and in five minutes you'll be climbing those little ledges with the dogs watching yhou. Keep your head—Theo's depending on you.

Four more steps. The rock walls were dry now, and the floor seemed to have levelled off. She wiped her palms down the sides of her jeans.

From the blackness ahead came the dull thud of a falling rock.

Paige stopped dead, her body ice-cold with fear. The roof was falling in. She would be trapped down here forever.

The silence screamed in her ears. Then, like a knife-blade drawn across her flesh, she heard the scrape of rock on rock. Someone—or something—was in the tunnel ahead of her. With a tiny moan of terror, she crumpled to the ground.

A light was shining in her eyes. Feebly, Paige pushed it away. Travis had shone a light in her eyes the first time she had met him . . .

Travis's voice said passionately and ungrammatically, 'Paige! Paige, darling, it's me—it's all right, we've found you. Please, Paige, say something!'

He was holding her in his arms, his breath stirring her cheek. He seemed to be waiting for a reply. 'It was you I heard,' she said weakly. 'I was so frightened——'

He hugged her hard against his chest. 'You're safe, sweetheart. Felix is with Theo right now. You were very brave to come down the mine, Paige.'

'I thought so, too,' she mumbled. 'What did you call me?'

There was a thread of laughter in his voice. 'Paige?'

'Before that.'

'Sweetheart?'

'And before that?'

'Darling.'

She burrowed into his shirtfront. 'So you don't mind that I came back?'

'I'm——'

Behind them someone cleared his throat. Felix said deprecatingly, 'Maybe we should try and get Theo out of here.'

'Theo can wait ten seconds,' Travis said, and kissed Paige.

It was a deliciously long ten seconds that, while it did not answer Paige's question, was nevertheless very satisfactory. When Travis finally released her, she tried to sit up and said meekly, 'Hello, Felix.'

Felix was carrying a flashlight with a very powerful beam. 'Welcome back,' he said.

Travis helped her to her feet. 'I was so worried about you—are you sure you're all right?'

Her knees were weak and her veins were singing with a dizzying mixture of hope and happiness. Trying to sound practical, Paige said, 'How are we going to get Theo out?'

The worst part was getting him up the ledges. But within half an hour Travis and Felix were carrying Theo in a fireman's lift down the mountain, Paige was carrying the flashlight, and the three dogs and the yellow-eyed wolf were trotting behind.

By the time the lights of the Camerons' house shone through the trees, Paige was ready for them. Both her hope and her happiness had dimmed, for she still had no real idea what Travis wanted; and the more they dimmed, the more her legs ached. When they all went in, Theo was naturally the centre of attention, although Nell did kiss her quickly on the cheek. As the men got him ready for bed, Nell bustled around preparing a compress for his ankle and hot chocolate for everyone.

Brent was asleep in the spare bed in Beth's room. Feeling redundant, Paige went in and sat down on the end of the bed, her shoulders bowed. Brent looked just the same, his brown curls tousled on the pillow and his small, steady breaths puffing in and out. Had he also missed her? she wondered. Would she be able to stay with him?

Travis blocked the doorway. 'Hot chocolate's ready, Paige.'

His voice gave nothing away. Obediently Paige went into the living-room, where the four of them talked about everything but Paige's mysterious return. Travis drained his mug and stood up. 'Can I leave Brent with you for the night?' he asked casually. 'I hate to wake him.'

'Sure,' said Felix.

Paige was still sitting at the table, clutching her mug as if she was afraid it was going to run away. Travis said just as casually, 'Coming, Paige?'

She got up. Two could play that game, she thought. 'I must say goodnight to Theo.'

Theo, tucked in bed, looked like a mischievous gnome. 'You and Travis leaving?' he said, far from quietly. 'Mind you talk some sense into him. Because there's got to be a wedding for you to get that ring—a proper wedding. You tell him that.'

'It's as well for you I already broke your flashlight,' Paige hissed. 'Or I might have been tempted to hit you on the head with it. Goodnight, Theo.'

Her cheeks were flushed when she left his room, and she was glad when she and Travis were finally alone on the path leading to his cabin. They walked in total silence, Travis striding along as if the devil was after him, Paige stubbornly determined not to ask him to slow down. Both hope and happiness had shrunk to almost nothing; and the void they had left had been filled with a paralysing fear.

Chimo and Minto greeted them as though they had been gone for days. Travis brushed them aside. He led the way into the cabin, lit the lamp, then finally turned to face Paige.

She jabbered, 'I'll go back first thing tomorrow. I can see you don't want me here, and I'm sorry if I embarrassed you in front of——'

His frown has been growing deeper with every word she spoke. 'While we were undressing Theo, he told me to be sure and ask you about the gold ring. What did he mean, Paige?'

'Theo is an interfering old busybody,' she snapped. 'He didn't mean anything of importance.'

'He also mentioned a wedding.'

She closed her eyes. 'Theo said he'd give me a pure gold ring if I married you,' she recited evenly. 'He was just talking nonsense, Travis—obviously there's to be no wedding.'

'Because you don't want to marry me.'

'Because *you* don't want to marry *me*,' she retorted, her eyes flying open.

'I never said that.'

'You didn't need to.'

He took a step closer. 'Why did you come back, Paige?'

She remembered Barbara's phrase, and said glibly, 'Unfinished business.'

'Related to Brent?'

Barbara's advice had been to take Travis to bed. Gazing into the inscrutable blue eyes, Paige decided instead, with a desperation born of having nothing to lose, to tell the truth. 'Related to you,' she said bluntly.

'Will you marry me, Paige?'

'Why should I?' she demanded.

'Because I love you more than anyone else in the world,' he said.

'That's no reason—*what* did you say?'

'You heard me.'

'You don't!'

He said drily, 'On matters of this importance, I endeavour to tell the truth. Particularly when it took me so long to figure it out. I knew from the first moment I saw you that I wanted you . . . but it took me longer to realise the reason I wanted you was because I loved you.' He hesitated, his face guarded again. 'Paige, do you love me?'

'Of course I do, I have for ages, how could I help it?' she cried. 'But *you* don't love me!'

Insensibly his features relaxed. 'Dearest Paige, I am trying very hard to keep my hands off you, because otherwise I'll be hauling you up those stairs to bed, and I feel we should attempt to settle this in some kind of rational way—but if you accuse me once more of not loving you, bed will win out. I don't know how else to convince you.'

She stared at him blankly. He did mean it. He did love her. He must. Or why else would he be talking this way? Suddenly she smiled, a smile as radiant as the morning sun. 'Travis,' she said, 'you don't love me.'

The blue eyes softened with laughter. He advanced on her, gathering her into his arms and carrying her up the stairs to his room. Pushing the door open with his knee, he went in and lowered her feet to the floor. 'Do you realise we've never made love in a bed, Paige Montgomery? Any bed. Let alone mine.'

Paige said, 'That could be remedied.' And then she said very little of anything for quite a while.

When next she spoke, their naked, satiated bodies were entwined on the bed, Travis leaned on one elbow as his fingers idly played with the short russet hair that curled about her ears. 'I'm convinced,' she said lazily.

'And is that all you have to say?'

Because she was very sensitive to his moods, she knew instinctively what he wanted. She said, her brown eyes bright with happiness, 'Travis, dear heart, I love you.'

He kissed her, his lips moving gently against hers. 'I had to wait a long time for that.'

Her hand was wrapped around his shoulder, bone and muscle and sinew; her fingers tightened in sudden possessiveness. She said spiritedly, 'You could have heard it four days ago if you'd asked me to stay. But you didn't. So I left, convinced you didn't love me.'

He said slowly, 'Did Pedro come back?'

'Pedro wasn't the real issue—I see that now.' Taking her time, Paige described what she had done in San Francisco, along with all the emotional nuances. 'It really was unfinished business . . .'

'Do you remember the day we made love on the mountain? I so nearly begged you to stay that day. But something stopped me, and I think it was the certainty that you had to settle your job and your brother's death on your own. I couldn't do it for you. In much the same way I had to learn I could write and still have time for a family . . . They've been hard lessons, haven't they?'

'So that was why you let me leave?' she asked in a small voice.

He stroked the line of her cheekbone. 'Maybe I should have asked you to marry me four days ago. But I was so angry with you after Barbara's phone call that I could hardly see straight. And, even less gloriously, I was afraid you'd say no. So I watched you leave, kicked myself around the block—metaphorically speaking—for the next two days, and was making plans to track you down in San Francisco. That was one of the reasons Brent and I went to Whitehorse.'

'You'd have come after me?' Paige said, enraptured.

'How could I not?' Travis's voice roughened. 'I want you as my wife, Paige. As mother of our children. Brent and our own.'

Tears sparkled on her lashes. 'That would make me happier than I ever thought I could be.'

He left a trail of kisses down her throat. 'Tomorrow we'll tell Theo we're holding him to his promise. I'll marry you with a ring of gold, Paige.'

She gathered him closer. 'I have to call Barbara tomorrow,

too, and tell her she's invited to a wedding.'

'And we'll have to tell Brent.'

Paige brought his hand to her breast. 'Lots to do,' she murmured.

'But in the meantime we have the cabin and the bed to ourselves, which may not happen again for a while—so I think we should take advantage of it. Would you agree?'

'Yes,' said Paige.

Harlequin *Presents*

Coming Next Month

1247 KING OF THE MOUNTAIN Melinda Cross
Ross Arnett is a superb fashion photographer He's also a good man in emergencies, as Marnie discovers when she has to follow him down a mountain in a blizzard.

1248 A SECURE MARRIAGE Diana Hamilton
Cleo proposes to her dynamic boss, Jude Mescal—not out of love, but in desperation. His surprising acceptance solves one of her problems but creates another For what can Jude possibly gain from their marriage?

1249 TUSCAN ENCOUNTER Madeleine Ker
Claudia buys the perfect farmhouse for herself and Vito, her fiancé, only to have the ownership disputed by the powerful Cesare di Stefano. The battle looms long and bitter until, among the verbal sparring, sparks of attraction start to fly

1250 NIGHT WITH A STRANGER Joanna Mansell
It's out of character for Lorel to blow a lot of money on a holiday But not as out of character as her behavior when she finds herself sitting beside Lewis Elliott on the Orient Express to Venice!

1251 A FEVER IN THE BLOOD Anne Mather
Cassandra flees to Italy and to Ben—the only person who can help her Then she realizes she's adding to her problems, not solving them, when the old attraction between them flares up again

1252 THE LOVE CONSPIRACY Susan Napier
Kate feels like a misfit in the life-style of her friend Todd's family, but resents their superior air She decides to teach them a lesson, especially Todd's uncle, Daniel Bishop—not knowing that she is the pawn in quite another game

1253 WILD ENCHANTMENT Kate Proctor
Jilly would never have told Jean-Luc de Sauvignet about her injury if she'd known that his doctorate wasn't in medicine But she had, and now it seems that with very little effort he can ruin her career— and happiness.

1254 FRIDAY'S CHILD Stephanie Wyatt
Mirry has misgivings about how Jay Elphick will fit into village life once he inherits Wenlow Hall—but she is prepared to welcome him She has no idea, though, just how much he holds their family past against her

Available in March wherever paperback books are sold, or through Harlequin Reader Service

In the U S.
901 Fuhrmann Blvd
P O Box 1397
Buffalo, N Y 14240-1397

In Canada
P O Box 603
Fort Erie, Ontario
L2A 5X3